倍斯特出版事業有限公司
Best Publishing Ltd.

新托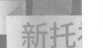

iBT
口說

MP3

韋爾 ◎ 著

《三大學習特色》

原文暢銷書神強化口說回答、
一次掌握六大類口說題型、強化逐步口譯實力

- 「**納入歷屆試題**」：精選最新20回TPO考題，掌握最新出題方向。
- 「**最充分備考**」：六種口說題型引導考生回答，考場應試時穩守25分。
- 「**優化表達**」：道地用字＋融入原文暢銷書內容，即刻提升口說分數至27⁺高分。

Author's Preface. 作者序

　　對於許多選擇要到國外留學的考生，對於雅思或新托福的名稱並不陌生，當中儘管測驗方式和題型不同，但要檢測的項目卻是相同的，在這兩項考試中均有聽、說、讀和寫。而「說」和「寫」對於亞洲考生來說，比起準備「聽」和「讀」相對吃力，在分數上也較難掌控。新托福中的寫作要以打字的方式進行，口說的部分則是不用面對考官直接以錄音的方式將答案講述出來（這對於不太習慣面對一個考官的考生來說是個優點，而且不用擔心太多，講就對了！），而雅思考試中的口說則需要面對一個考官，以面對面的方式進行三個part的測驗，在寫作部分，則需要以手寫的方式完成兩個part的測驗題型。

　　其實不管測驗進行的方式為何，在這兩個考試中，我們都能從歷屆官方試題（新托福的TPO或雅思的劍橋雅思系列）找得出蛛絲馬跡，考的內容都是一個生活中常見的主題，要考生進行論述或提出看法，而要考到一定分數除了要掌握一定水平的文法、字彙量、道地用語等，更重要的是要有內容、與眾不同等等（表達的太general或語句redundant都是扣分的原因）。有內容且表達具

體的口說答案則需要一定的閱讀量才能將答案答好。

　　閱讀是一切的基石，例如在表達財富或理財看法的題目中，有看過相關書籍像是《窮爸爸富爸爸》或是《有錢人想的跟你不一樣》這兩本書的考生，在雅思口說part 2或3或是新托福的口說中就能很自然地講出不一樣的論點，且讓自己的論述更有根據和更believable，就像是在簡報或辯論中，除了一些技巧表達外，你真的很需要hard facts輔助你的論點。

　　如果是一般口說或求職口試，可能還可以再講些更不一樣的書籍，例如《巴比倫最富有的人》、《原來有錢人都這麼做》和《我用死薪水輕鬆理財賺千萬》，因為有時候求職者眾，可能太多人都看過《窮爸爸富爸爸》，在條件相差不多的情況下，多些不一樣的答案，往往會有更意想不到的效果，讓自己更脫穎而出。

　　在雅思和新托福的口說和寫作中更是如此，考官要閱的卷、面試的人、聽的音檔相當多，有些答案聽膩了，能更表達出個人化的表達，就能獲取更高分。

在新托福口説這本書中，納入了更道地和生活化的表達，有的答案融入電影人物和一些暢銷書籍，有這些佳句的襯托後，更能讓考官有更不一樣的感受，而不是只是聽到死板板、冰冷的模板答法。考生除了從中學習外，可以構思自己的答題思路並找外籍友人等練習，讓答案更自然，在應考時能像平常聊天那樣答出六個part的答案。最後要感謝倍斯特出版給予本人出書的機會，以及祝所有考生都能獲取理想成績。

韋爾 敬上

Editor's Preface. 編者序

　　新托福口説包含了六個不同類型的口説問題，對於亞洲考生來説是個蠻大的考驗，可能因為我們都習慣了別人詢問一個問題，然後我們回答對方問題的測驗模式。雖然前兩個類型的口説問題和後四個看似迴異，其實在答這幾個不同類型的問題時，只要轉換思考方式，都是等同於前兩個類型的口説問題。我們只需要把它想成是在前兩個類型中加入了其他元素，例如聽一段短對話、閱讀一段文章等等。仿佛像是製作蛋糕那樣，我們其實會製作，只是有的蛋糕必須是客製化的、有的需要淋上幾層糖霜或是做些小改變，只是我們還不熟悉這些模式。如果把口説測驗的六道題目以這樣的方式來想並熟悉這六個題型的測驗方式後就會覺得，其實真的沒有什麼唉。

　　例如，part 3的口説測驗題型好了（包含了**看一段短文＋聽一段短對話＋以口説表達觀點**），像極了學校附近要開一間咖啡館了，無

聊之中走到系辦前的公告欄，看了一段文字，然後在電梯口聽到其他一對男女講述關於新咖啡館開幕的一小段話，爾後自己在等的人（可能是閨密、男朋友或女朋友）出現了，自己理所當然的把看到的公告欄跟剛聽到的話，整合成自己和對方的聊天內容。其實part 3的口説模式就是這樣，你用更放鬆的心情去看待，多練習和聽短對話時把筆記記好就可以囉，別想成是在寫TPO試題或是準備考試，這樣會讓自己心情更緊繃更講不好。也可以試試在校園網站上看到一段內容和聽到幾個朋友在臉書等平台分享心情後，找個外籍友人喝杯咖啡，用英文簡短的講出要描述的部分，這些都能無形中增加應考時更平穩的表現。又或是part 5的口説題好了，把它想成跟自己生活相關的話題

（像是書中提到的scheduling conflict話題）自己是大四生，但其實都一直把重心放在求職，也有參加航空公司面試，如果其中一輪的面試日期跟大肆下學期其中一門課的期中考或期末考的日期衝突時，自己會怎麼做？自己只是聽一段這樣的短對話，聽兩個人描述這樣的情況，作好筆記並提出自己的看法。其他幾個part的測驗方式也可以用這樣的方式轉換心情去答題，效果會很不同喔！最後祝所有考生都能取得理想成績。

倍斯特編輯部 敬上

Instructions 使用說明

🗣 回說回答

Unit 4 感到最享受的交通工具
— TPO 47 Task 1

請先別看後面的參考答案，先自己練習一次，看自己聽到問題會如何回答這題，練習過後，可以參考書中三個回答，並將佳句記下和觀看解析，用於應考中，更無往不利的應考。

_____
_____
_____
_____
_____
_____
_____
_____
_____
_____

(Prepare time: 15 seconds，Response time: 45 seconds)

新托福口說「第一類」的題型：個人喜好題

· 在聽完試題後，會有15秒的準備時間和**45**秒的作答時間。務必練習在這樣的秒數內達到一定量的表達句數。

· 屬於聽一段試題描述後的答題，牽涉到聽和說，是考生較熟悉的模式。

😊 一問三答 ▶MP3 008

❶ Trains

Trains of course. Taking a train makes you relaxed during the journey of the trip, and you get to see all the beautiful scenery passing by in swift review. In addition, you have plenty of time to do your own thing. Things have always been hectic with work and love life and so on…sitting on the train, you eventually have a little time to reflect on things happening lately to see if there is anything you did wrong or to figure out how to avoid an embarrassing situation. Plus, sometimes an idea pops out of nowhere…it's amazing actually.

當然是火車囉!旅程途中期間搭火車讓你感到放鬆，而且你能看到美麗的景色很快速的映入眼簾。此外，你有許多時間做自己要做的事。總是因為工作和感情生活等等的事感到忙亂…坐在火車內，你最終有點時間去思考最近所發生的事情，看是否你有做錯的或了解如何避免一場令人感到尷尬的情況。再者，有時候一個想法不知道從哪蹦出…這實令人感到吃驚。

❷ Bicycles

Unit 4 感到最享受的交通工具
— TPO 47 Task 1

I would definitely choose the bicycle. The enjoyment of taking a bicycle is beyond anything. Exercising pacifies your mind and burns extra calories. In addition, exercising eases your stress and it is especially helpful when you take a bike to work. Even though you have to like go an extraordinary length to take an extra suit to work and change it, you can totally feel like Sandra Bullock in the Proposal. The benefits of the morning exercise is just beyond description. Of course, you have to experience it to realize that it's true. I guess people might change their perception and choose bicycling, too.

我確定會選擇腳踏車。搭乘腳踏車的享受超過任何事情。運動緩和心智而且燃燒額外的卡路里。此外，運動舒緩你的壓力而且對於騎乘腳踏車上班的人來說特別有幫助。即使你必須要大費周張攜帶額外的套裝到工作場合並做更換，你可以全然感到像是在「愛情限時簽」電影中珊卓布拉克那樣。晨間運動的益處超乎於你能想像的。當然，你必須要經歷過後才能體會到它的真實性。我想人們可能會改變他們的觀點，也改選擇腳踏車呢?

35

一問三答 ▶MP3 018

① Save the extra money

Of course, the answer is to save the extra money. Remember the old wisdom from *The Richest Man in Babylon*, money comes to those who save it. Frittering away with the money can only give you the transient pleasure, but once the excitement goes away, you are right back to where you are. A one-time lottery winner can lose lots of money in a short time and be seen living under a bridge of the freezing winter night, let alone the person who earns a fixed income. In addition, you just don't know what life is going to test you. Without the saving, you will regret when something bad happens to you.

當然，答案是存下額外的錢。記得「巴比倫最富有的人」裡頭的古老智慧吧？，金錢來自於那些將它存下者，揮霍浪費掉金錢只會便你獲得短暫的樂趣，但是一旦那種興奮感消退，你馬上有回到本來到的狀態。曾經的樂透得主可能在橋下住者，更別說去許多錢，然後於寒冷的冬天夜晚被發現在橋下住者，更別說是只賺取固定薪資者，此外，你就是不會知道生命在未來考驗著你什麼。沒有了存款，你會在厄運來臨時後悔莫及。

66

③ spend it right away

Spend it right away…since I'm not planning to have kids, start a family, buy a house, and so on. Why can't I just spend all the extra money…and to be honest, saving for the rainy day thing is an old concept…you just have to let go of it. In life, you can't even know what's going to happen to you in the next second. No one knows…even the fortune-teller does not. So I definitely will be the kind of the person who cherishes every moment and enjoys every moment of life…and of course with the EXTRA MONEY.

馬上花掉…既然我不打算要有小孩，成家立業，買房了等等的，為什麼我不能花掉所有額外的金錢吧，而且說實話，未雨綢繆是老舊的觀點了…你就是該放掉這個觀點了。在生命中，你甚至無法得知下一秒你會發生什麼事…沒有人知道…甚至算命師都不知道。所以我肯定是那種珍惜每個當下的人，而且享受生命中每個時刻…當然附帶著會用掉額外的金錢。

68

② Save the extra money

Save the extra money. I'm an advocate of living your life to the fullest, and like everyone once in a while I do indulge myself with a little shopping and international trips. But that money is not from my payment, my fixed income. It's from the house rent every month I receive, and you can't spend your fixed income on luxuries and international trips. You can only use your bonuses, investment mo… from the stock market, or house rent you receive… …leasure. **So saving money**… …… At tha…

存……
者，而……
旅行，……
是來自……
入花掉……
股市等……
到樂趣……
實。

UNIT 1 Restriction of Cycling on Campus
禁止在校內騎自行車

Narrator: you will now read a short passage on a campus situation and then listen to a talk on that same subject. Then you will be asked to answer a question from both the reading and the talk. After the question you will have 30 seconds to prepare and 60 seconds to respond. ▶MP3 033

Narrator: Best University is now debating about whether cycling on campus is too dangerous, especially after the accident. Read the article from the local newspaper, written by a news reporter. You will have 45 seconds to read the article. Begin reading now.

Reading time: 45 seconds

Simply put…there is no way that Best University will allow students to ride bicycles in the school…after an accident happened the other day…a student's hand was severely injured…and is still unconscious in the hospital…there are still some reporters waiting outside the ICU 2…to see how parents are going to respond to the accident. There are simply too many meandering routes from school districts to districts… it's like bicycle racing contest and pedestrians are sometimes competing with bicycle riders for the road. Wow…that student has no intention of slowing down at the turn…which is pretty scary…it seems that Best University needs to take drastic measures to counter with the safety of bicycle riding in the campus…and the vote for "Restriction of Cycling on Campus" is this Wednesday…3 p.m.

01 個人喜好
02 二選一題組
03 描述觀點
04 整合文章和講座
05

Narrator: now listen to two students discussing the article. ▶MP3 034

⭐ **筆記**

_____
_____
_____
_____
_____
_____

👄 **回說回答**

The woman expresses her opinion about **Restriction of Cycling on Campus.** State her opinion and explain the reasons she gives for that opinion. ▶MP3 035

Prepare time: 30 seconds
Response time: 60 seconds

新托福口說「第三類」的題型：概述觀點

- 在聽完試題後，會有 30 秒的準備時間和 **60** 秒的作答時間。務必練習在這樣的秒數內達到一定量的表達句數。

- 與前兩類型的題目不同的是，這部分的題型，在聽完題目指示後，會需要先閱讀一小段文章（有 45 秒的時間可以閱讀該文章），閱讀後接著會聆聽一段短對話，聽對話人物描述該情況，接著考生整合閱讀和聽力訊息後提供答案，當中牽涉到「閱讀」→「聽力」→「口說」，考生 可以多練習並適應這樣的答題模式。

筆記

- 請務必在聆聽短對話時記下重點，並將重點消化後，以口述方式答完這題。

短對話

- 若對於聽一段短對話後，未能掌握對話重點並回答該題，請以短對話內容做影子跟讀練習，先多強化聽力後再寫試題或演練 TPO。

- 練習這類試題時，須建立在具備一定閱讀和聽力基礎上才能答好。

- 如果還有更多備考時間，可以以短對話中譯練習口譯，可以大幅強化這個類型和後面幾個類型的答題能力喔！

Jim: have you seen the news yet?

Cindy: what…the news of the accident?

Jim: pretty horrible…even though I don't know him… but looking at the screenshot of him lying in the hospital…I think we should vote against Cycling on Campus…

Cindy: how did that happen…I thought you can't film or take photos in the ICU room…

Jim: perhaps they pay handsomely to get that shot… but that's not the main focus here…

Cindy: I feel bad that he got injured…but what about convenience? And the person who follows strict guidelines given during the announcement of the freshman campus tour…and the campus is just so big…and I'm not a marathon runner…I don't think I will vote against it…

118

參考答案

- 請務必自己回答過後再觀看參考答案喔，這樣才不會降低應考時的反應力。

According to the report, we are uncertain about how schools are going to respond, but it seems that the vote will be the determining factor for whether cycling will be allowed on campus or not. The woman feels bad about the accident happening, but at the same time pinpoints something like convenience, and students who follow the rules. It may be unfair for someone who follows the rules while riding a bike. Also, she mentions that the campus is too big for students. She will not vote against Cycling on Campus…

根據報導，我們對於學校會如何反應是不確定的，但是似乎投票會是校內是否允許騎乘腳踏車的決定性因素。女生對於事件的發生感到難過，但同時也指出一些像是便利性、遵守規定的學生。可能對於某些遵守規定的騎乘者是不公平的。而且，她提到學校對於學生來說太大了。她不會對騎乘腳踏車一事投反對票。

120

Unit 1 Restriction of Cycling on Campus 禁止在校內騎自行車

- 將短對話中文以英文口譯出來。

吉姆： 你看到新聞了嗎？

辛蒂： 什麼…意外事件那則新聞嗎？

吉姆： 相當恐怖…即使我不認識他…但是看著他躺在病床上的截圖…我認為我們對於校園騎乘腳踏車一事應該要投反對票。

辛蒂： 那是怎麼發生的…我以為在加護病房裡你不能攝影或拍照…

吉姆： 或許他們付了可觀的金額才拿到那樣子的照片…但是這不是討論的重點。

辛蒂： 對於他受傷的部分我感到難過…但是關於腳踏車的便利性呢？而且嚴格遵守在大一新生校園導覽時的公告的騎乘者？校園這麼大…還有我不是馬拉松跑者…我不認為我會投反對票。

│01 惱人喜好
│02 「三重」話題
│03 概述觀點
│04 整合文章和講座
│05 討論解決辦法
│06 概述講座內容

121

11

UNIT 4

invasive species
外來物種－福壽螺

Narrator: you will now read a short passage and then listen to a talk on the same academic topic. You will then be asked a question about them. After you hear the question, you will have 30 seconds to prepare your response and 60 seconds to speak.

Narrator: now read the passage about **invasive species**. You will have 45 seconds to read the passage. Begin reading now. ▶ MP3 065

Reading time: 45 seconds

Invasive Species

In biology, an invasive species refers to a non-native species, a species not native to a certain place. Sometimes it is accidentally introduced by humans through air travel. Other time, it is deliberately introduced. Whatever the reasons behind the introduction, an invasive species can cause unseen damage to a certain geographical location, and the damage is beyond our control. It is quite tenacious and it can thrive in that location for quite well. Under most circumstances, they have no natural enemies in the location.

Narrator: now listen to part of a lecture on this topic in a biology class. ▶ MP3 066

☆ 筆記

_____
_____
_____
_____
_____

👄 口說回答

Explain how the example from the professor's lecture tells us more about the non-native species.
▶ MP3 067

筆記

· 請務必在聆聽短對話時記下重點，並將重點消化後，以口述方式答完這題。

新托福口說「第四類」的題型：
整合文章與講座

· 在聽完試題後，會有 30 秒的準備時間和 **60 秒**的作答時間。務必練習在這樣的秒數內達到一定量的表達句數。

· 這部分的題型與「第三類」題目的作答時間和答題模式相同，在聽完題目指示後，會需要先閱讀一小段文章（有45秒的時間可以閱讀該文章），閱讀後接著會聆聽一段講座 (lecture)，接著考生整合閱讀和聽力訊息後提供答案，當中牽涉到「閱讀」→「聽力」→「口說」，差異點在於聽講座的部分，講座話題比起短對話來說，會較難或生澀，考生可以多練習這類型的題目，並作大量 TPO 練習，提升聽講座內容的能力。

聽力原文 和中譯

Non-native or as we call them non-indigenous species are hard to get rid of since they do not have natural enemies. Golden apple snails are a well-known non-indigenous species in Taiwan. They possess traits of non-native species, such as fast growth and rapid reproduction. They are omnivores and tend to eat the tender parts of plants, such as the stems and leaves. They are doing quite a lot of damage to rice fields and potatoes by the river bank. Harvests of agricultural crops are heavily influenced by the presence of the golden apple snails. Other Asian countries have also suffered from the harm caused by the golden apple snails. Luckily, people have come up with ways to cope with overpopulation of the golden apple snails. Fish have been used as a way to combat the golden apple snail invasion, although not as useful as fresh-water turtles. Several species of turtles can be more effective in controlling the population of golden apple snails. What's more interesting is that ducks can be used for controlling the species. Another less well-known species, the African sacred ibis also can be used to decrease the number of the species. The funny thing is they are non-native species as well. It's like using non-native species to control another non-indigenous species.

非本土的物種或者是我們所稱的非原生的物種很難移除，因為它們沒有天敵。金蘋果蝸牛在台灣一直是因非原生種而聞名。它們擁有非本土物種的特質，例如快速生長和快速繁衍。它們是雜食性動物，而且傾向食用植物柔嫩部位，例如莖和葉子。它們對於稻田和河岸邊的馬鈴薯造成了相當的損害。農作物的收成成果大幅地受到金蘋果蝸牛的影響。其他亞洲國家也遭受到金蘋果蝸牛的危害。幸運地是，人們已經想出處理金蘋果蝸牛的過度成長問題。魚類已經用於對抗金蘋果郭牛的入侵，儘管沒有比淺水水域的烏龜有效。有些烏龜能夠有效的控制金蘋果蝸牛的族群。另一個較不知名的物種，非洲聖鷺也能用於降低這個物種的數量。有趣的是它們也不是本土物種。這像是使用非本土物種去控制另一個非原生物種。

回說回答 和中譯　▶MP3 068

In describing the non-native species, the professor uses a more well-known species to explain the concept. Golden apple snails have been a more well-known non-native species to us since high school, and are the non-native species here in Taiwan. Throughout the entire lecture, we can easily grasp two major traits of non-native species, fast growth and rapid reproduction. Golden apple snails possess those and they are causing quite a damage to agricultural crops, even in some Asian countries. Luckily, people have come up with ways to use other species to control the overpopulation of the golden apple snails. Species, such as fish, turtles, and even ducks, and non-native species, African sacred ibis.

在描述非本土物種時，教授使用了較知名的物種去解釋這個概念。金蘋果蝸牛一直是自從高中後，較知名的非本土物種，而且在台灣也是非本土物種。透過整個講課，我們可以輕易地掌握兩個主要而且非本土物種的特徵，快速生長和快速繁殖。金蘋果蝸牛擁有那些而且它們導致農作物相當程度的危害，甚至是在一些亞洲國家。幸運地是，人們已經想出方法，使用其他物種來控制金蘋果蝸牛的族群過度成長。物種，例如魚類、烏龜和甚至是鴨子和非本土物種，非洲聖鷺。

整合能力強化

· 使用口說題「閱讀」原文強化「寫作」能力。

在生物學中，外來種指的是非本土的物種，不是原產於本地的物種。有時候會不經意由人們透過航空旅行引進。在其他時候，是有意引進。不論引進背後的原因為何，外來種能導致特定地域未能察覺被覺的損害，而這損害是超過我們所能控制的。這物種是相當頑強的而且能夠在那個地方繁殖起來。在大多數的情況下，它們在該地區沒有天敵。

_____
_____
_____
_____
_____
_____

參考答案

· 請務必自己回答過後再觀看參考答案喔，這樣才不會降低應考時的反應力。

講座內容

· 這部分較需要多花心思，因為較難遇到已經熟悉的學術話題或考題與本身主修相關。建議可以多練習這樣長度的內容和寫 TPO 試題。

· 此外，可以使用聽力原文中譯練習口譯（或閱讀文章中譯練習寫作），同步強化口說（或寫作）表達和提升應答第四類題型的能力。

新托福口說「第五類」的題型：
討論解決方法

· 在聽完試題後，會有 20 秒的準備時間和 **60 秒的作答時間**。務必練習在這樣的秒數內達到一定量的表達句數。

· 「第五類」和「第六類」的準備時間和作答時間是一樣的。

· 這部分題型，在聽完題目指示後，會需要聆聽一段「短對話」，接著考生整合聽力訊息後提供答案，當中僅牽涉到「聽力」→「口說」。比較需要注意的部分是摘要訊息和記筆記等能力，並即刻想出其中哪個解決方法較佳和解釋為什麼。其實放鬆心情反而能答好這題。常看歐美影集者，在這類型的答題上會覺得極容易，但在聽時則需要非常專注和降低自己口語表達時的文法錯誤即可。

參考答案

· 請務必自己回答過後再觀看參考答案喔，這樣才不會降低應考時的反應力。

 參考答案 ▶MP3 078

The woman is having a scheduling conflict. Her interview at ABC Airline and her final exam are on the same date. There are two possible solutions in the conversation. The first solution is that she can talk to the professor to see if she can take the test on another day. The second solution is risky. She can take a taxi right after the interview. I would recommend the second solution because I have a very similar experience before, and normally professors are willing to arrange another day for you. And imagine how hard it is to eventually go to the third round. The second solution is too risky, so I won't recommend the second one. You can blow either one.

女子有時程衝突的問題。她在ABC航空公司的面試和她的期末考試在同一天。在會話中有著兩個可能的解決方案。第一個解決方案是她可以與教授談談，看是否能讓她在其他天考試。第二個解決方案是有風險的。她可以在面試後搭計程車。我會建議第二個解決方案因為我之前有著非常相同的經驗，而通常教授會願意替你安排另一天考試。而且很難想像要多努力才能進到第三輪的面試。第二個解決方案太冒險了，所以我不會建議第二個解決方案。妳會搞砸其中一件事。

232

 整合能力強化

· 重新聽一次對話並將內容默寫

01 個人

默出所有短對話內容

· 可以要求自己聽新托福口說或聽力試題或聽一段短對話時，**聽兩次後將所有訊息全默寫出**，會大幅提升聽力實力喔！其實在有些較要求的外文系課程或大一和大二英文課程有些老師會這樣要求。其實經過這樣的訓練一段時間後，會覺得答新多益聽力等對話式聽力，不需要很費力聽都能輕鬆答對聽力試題，可以多試試喔！

新托福口說「第六類」的題型：摘要講座內容

· 在聽完試題後，會有 20 秒的準備時間和 **60** 秒的作答時間。

· 這部分題型，在聽完題目指示後，會需要聆聽一段「**短篇講座**」，接著考生整合聽力訊息後提供答案，當中僅牽涉到「**聽力**」「**口說**」，差別在這部分是聽短篇講座，而第五類型的題目是聽一段短對話，也要特別注意摘要訊息和記筆記等能力，講座內容有時候不是自己熟悉的主題時，就容易失分，建議要多練習TPO 試題。

· 另外，可以以聽力原文進行**口譯**或**筆譯**練習，強化自己的口說和寫作能力。

Contents 目次

Part 3 概述觀點題

Part 6 概括講座內容題

part **1**

個人喜好題

個人喜好題精選了 8 個主題提供考生練習，包含了一份特別的禮物、工作求職、學習方式、交通、個人規劃、個人特質、學習成長和工作話題，每個回答均提供三個選擇答案，可以於練習和參考完三個答案後，構思出自己的回答，實際演練過後在考試時，答題會更流暢。

1 一份特別的禮物
曾收到或贈送給人的最棒的特別禮物

Narrator: You will now be asked a question about a familiar topic. After you read the question, you will have 15 seconds to prepare your response and 45 seconds to speak.

Task 1 Best special gift ever received or gave someone
▶ **MP3 001**

回說 回答

請先別看後面的參考答案，自己練習一次，看自己聽到問題會如何回答這題，練習過後，可以參考書中三個回答，並將佳句記下和觀看解析，用於應考中，更無往不利。

_____

_____

_____

_____

_____

_____

_____

_____

_____

_____

(Prepare time: 15 seconds，Response time: 45 seconds)

PART 01 個人喜好

PART 02 二選一話題

PART 03 概述觀點

PART 04 整合文章和講座

PART 05 討論解決辦法

PART 06 概括講座內容

❶ the letter from my grandparents

The special gift was a letter from my grandparents. It's not so much the letter itself as words of wisdom from my grandparents. They listed the kind of the predicament I am going to face in the following twenty years. It was written in cursive writing of course, and looks pretty tattered. **It's like the prophecy of my life in the next two decades, totally looks like the clay tablet in *The Richest Man in Babylon.*** Since it was too invaluable, I used to put it in the safe, and now I'm handling it to my kid…kind of reminding them the gestures from their great grandparents, and would like them to pass on to their kids and so on.

特別的禮物是一封我祖父母給的信。與其說是信件本身不如說是我祖父母身上的智慧之語。他們列出了我在接下來20年將面臨到的問題。而當然是以英文草寫書寫成的，看起來相當殘破。它像是我接下來20幾年生活的預言，完全像是在「巴比倫最富有的人」書中的泥土碑。既然它無比昂貴，我過去將它放在保險櫃裡頭，而現在我將信件轉交到我小孩身上...有點像是提醒他們這是他們曾祖父的好意，也想要他們將這個傳到他們小孩身上等等的。

❷ A powerful weapon in the on-line game

A powerful weapon in the online game. It might seem so bizarre…I know…but to game lovers, it is so special. In the fictional world, **players are also perceived by the weapon you have.** People want to team up with the person who possesses the powerful weapon and knows how to play the game. But accumulating a certain amount of money to buy that takes quite some time, and ever since I knew a friend of mine would like to have powerful weapons, I thought when one day I had a much powerful one, I would give the powerful weapon to my friend. So I give it to him as his birthday present. **Of course, he wrote something on his Facebook wall "best special gift ever received."**

線上遊戲中強大的武器。我知道…這可能令人感到很奇怪…但是對遊戲愛好者，這份禮物是很特別的。在虛構世界裡，玩家的價值是由你所擁有的武器來評價的。人們想要與擁有強大武器且知道如何玩遊戲的人組隊。但是累積到特定額的金錢去購買要花費相當多的時間，而且自從我知道我一位朋友想要有強大的武器時，我思考著有天我有更強的武器時，我要把我強大的武器給我朋友。所以我把武器給他當作他的生日禮物。當然他在他的臉書牆上寫道：「所收到的最棒的特別禮物」。

❸ An electronic card of the country club

The most special gift I gave to my friend is an electronic card of the country club. You know how expensive that is, but **the gift just stood out from the rest** in his promotion party. Since my friend just loves to play golf so much, I bought the electronic card of the country club for him so that he can play golf for free…. and during the five-year period. Partly to thank him for my breast cancer surgery. He was the doctor. **Compared with my life, it is just a small way for me to say thank you.**

　　我給我朋友最特別的禮物是鄉村俱樂部的電子感應卡。你知道它有多昂貴，但是在他升遷派對上，**這份禮物從所有禮物中超群絕倫**。因為我朋友就是很喜愛玩高爾夫球，我購買了鄉村俱樂部的電子感應卡給他，這樣一來他就能免費玩高爾夫球了…在五年使用期限內。部分是想感謝他替我動的乳癌外科手術。他是手術的醫生。**比起我的生命來說，這僅是我很些微的方式去表達出對他的感謝。**

解析

　　這個單元的談話是要求考生講述一個自己曾收到或贈送給人的最棒的特別禮物。在考試當下，應立即想出自己要描述的禮物是什麼，並想好幾個論述點或形容詞，在接下來的回答中可以使用上。第一個回答除了有鋪陳式的回答外，祖父母給的信也令人耳目一新。另外，融入了「巴比倫最富有的人」增添聽者的興趣。Totally look like等表達也讓聽者不會覺得像是唸稿等感覺，而更像是在與人對話時講的話。

　　第二個回答除了很反映出年輕世代外，語氣表達等也像是在講話，最後的「當然他在他的臉書牆上寫道：...」讓口說表達更活潑和令人感到印象深刻。

　　第三個回答很豪華版，但是後面使用的語氣、表達和感謝等，都讓人感到溫馨，是個有溫度的回答。三個答案都有很多值得學習的句型，除了能用於收到或給對方最特別的禮物的話題外，也能用在其他類似的口說話題中喔！

PART 01 個人喜好

PART 02 二選一話題

PART 03 概述觀點

PART 04 整合文章和講座

PART 05 討論解決辦法

PART 06 概括講座內容

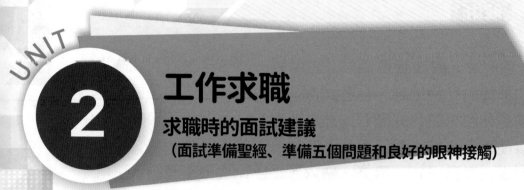

UNIT 2 工作求職
求職時的面試建議
（面試準備聖經、準備五個問題和良好的眼神接觸）

Narrator: You will now be asked a question about a familiar topic. After you read the question, you will have 15 seconds to prepare your response and 45 seconds to speak.

Task 1 Your suggestions for a job interview. Use specific examples and details to support your opinion.
▶ **MP3 003**

口說 回答

請先別看後面的參考答案，自己練習一次，看自己聽到問題會如何回答這題，練習過後，可以參考書中三個回答，並將佳句記下和觀看解析，用於應考中，更無往不利。

_____

_____

_____

_____

_____

_____

_____

_____

(Prepare time: 15 seconds，Response time: 45 seconds)

PART 01 個人喜好

PART 02 二選一話題

PART 03 概述觀點

PART 04 整合文章和講座

PART 05 討論解決辦法

PART 06 概括講座內容

 ▶MP3 004

❶ Knock'em Dead

Knock'em Dead, of course, it's like the basic before going to an interview. I just can't imagine why some people go to an interview without preparing interview questions from *Knock'em Dead*. It's like you are not well-prepared, and often you can blow the chance for your desired job and regret from ten years on that I wish I had prepared those questions. In life, you cannot bear too many regrets. **One would be fine. More than one would definitely be so inexcusable. You are throwing your life away and often there is no second chance in life.**

　　當然是*Knock'em Dead*啊，這像是參加面試前的基本準備。我真的無法想像有些人去參加面試，絲毫無準備*Knock'em Dead*裡的面試問題。這就像是你沒準備好，通常你會搞砸你想要的工作機會，而且十年後後悔著但願我當時有準備那些問題。在生命中，你就是不能承受那麼多的遺憾。一個可能還好。超過一個遺憾絕對是無法被寬容的。你正將丟棄生命中的機會，而通常生命中沒有第二次機會。

❷ be well-prepared + prepare five questions

Be well-prepared. I know…to be well-prepared is like a cliché, but often interviewees misunderstand what that means. So be well-prepared…sorry I have to say the word a little louder. Buying yourself a decent suit and making you look like a clean-cut person are just a part of it. You also need to study intensely about the corporate cultures and prepare at least five questions you would like to ask after the interviewer asks you do you have any questions?, probably at the end of the interview. Often everything goes too smooth and then most interviewees just blow on this one. **I just can't believe some candidates stand out from the rest are the ones who have prepared those questions. So PREPARE FIVE QUESTIONS.**

完善的準備。我知道…完善的準備像是陳腔濫調，但是通常面試者誤會了這個意思。所以要完善準備…抱歉我必須將這個字說的更大聲些。買個像樣的西裝而且讓你自己看起來乾乾淨淨的僅是準備的一部分。你也需要深入研究公司文化和至少準備五個問題，在面試者詢問你「你還有任何問題嗎？」時，可以問對方，很可能是在面試最後的階段。通常事情都進行得太順利，然後大多數的面試者就搞砸了這個問題。**我真的不敢相信有些面試者從競爭中鶴立雞群僅因為他們有準備那些問題。所以準備五個問題吧！**

01 個人喜好　PART

02 二選一話題　PART

03 概述觀點　PART

04 整合文章和講座　PART

05 討論解決辦法　PART

06 概括講座內容　PART

❸ Good Eye contact

Good eye contact. Definitely the most important one. **Most of human interactions rest on good eye contact.** Interviewers are looking at you to see if you are confident enough, or whether you are certain about the thing you just said, or whether you are telling them the truth, and **sometimes trust comes from having good eye contact.** From my experience as an HR manager, interviewees who maintain good eye contact generally leave a good impression, and therefore they are deemed as trustworthy and honest, and of course they stand out from the rest. So don't be afraid of looking into the eyes of an interviewer.

良好的眼神接觸。確定是最重要的一個。**大多數人類互動是仰賴良好的眼神接觸。**面試者看著你檢視著你是否有足夠的自信或是你是否很確定你自己所講述的話，或你是否是講實話，而且**有時候信賴來自於有良好的眼神接觸。**從我當人事經理的經驗，面試者們能維持良好的眼神接觸，一般來說都能留下良好的印象，因此他們被認定為值得信賴且誠實的，而且理所當然的他們從其他競爭者中勝出。所以別害怕看著面試官的眼睛。

解析

　　這個單元的談話是要求考生提供一個求職時的面試建議。第一個回答很實用，明確指出要如何才能達到目的，也列舉了 *Knock'em Dead* 這本書，利用實用性且充分準備就能替面試加到分，後面比較是閒聊，讓人有輕鬆的感覺，像是在與考官聊天互動，不是死記答案。

　　第二個答案也蠻不錯的，中間也使用讓考官不會覺得是背答案的回答，包含…is like a cliché和…sorry I have to say the word a little louder等等，是個讓人覺得輕鬆的回答。

　　第三個是題到良好的眼神接觸，前面使用簡短的回答，像是在對話中常見的話語，然後融入實用的建議，最後講明為什麼這點很重要，是個實用的好回答。其實關於工作面試的部分建議有超多喔，不只這三個回答所列出來的，考生可以收集好資料後融入自己的想法在裡頭，在考試中使用。

PART 01 個人喜好

PART 02 二選一話題

PART 03 概述觀點

PART 04 整合文章和講座

PART 05 討論解決辦法

PART 06 概括講座內容

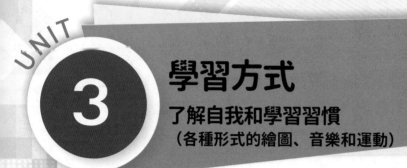

學習方式

了解自我和學習習慣
（各種形式的繪圖、音樂和運動）

Narrator: You will now be asked a question about a familiar topic. After you read the question, you will have 15 seconds to prepare your response and 45 seconds to speak.

Task 1 Figure out what method works best for you is the key. Explain your study habits.

▶ **MP3 005**

🗨️ 回說 回答

請先別看後面的參考答案，自己練習一次，看自己聽到問題會如何回答這題，練習過後，可以參考書中三個回答，並將佳句記下和觀看解析，用於應考中，更無往不利。

_____

_____

_____

_____

_____

_____

_____

_____

_____

_____

(Prepare time: 15 seconds，Response time: 45 seconds)

PART 01 個人喜好

PART 02 二選一話題

PART 03 概述觀點

PART 04 整合文章和講座

PART 05 討論解決辦法

PART 06 概括講座內容

❶ Different drawings

Different drawings. I have different drawings for various subjects. **I can visualize the concept from just viewing it, and it's quite effective.** In biology, different charts explain relationships among different animals, whereas in history, different charts elucidate historical events chronologically. It's like cracking the code for each test, and I won't have to recite as hard as my classmates. Sometimes they just wonder how I prepare all those tests in less time, and **their bewilderment increases after I get an exceedingly high SAT score.** I guess you just have to figure out what method works best for you.

不同的繪畫。對於不同的學科我會繪製不同的圖。**僅靠觀看圖示，我能將概念形象化，而且成效相當好。**在生物學，不同的圖形解釋不同動物間的關係，而在歷史課，不同的圖形以時間順序解釋歷史事件。這就像是破解每個考試一樣，而且我不需要像我同班同學那樣背的很費力。有時候他們會想我是如何在較少時間內準備好所有那些考試，而且**他們的困惑，隨著我拿到異常高分的SAT分數而增加。**我想你必須要了解哪個方法對你來說最合適。

❷ Music

Music is quite soothing. Listening to soft music while studying is the key to my academic success, and **the idea comes from the English teaching theory, suggestopedia. I actually adapted it into another form. Listening to foreign music accelerates my pace of accommodating into other language settings.** The music of other foreign languages just reverberates in my mind, and I effortlessly pass my French and Russian courses. I guess the most important thing about studying is to know your learning style first so that you will pick up the rhythm really quick and have enough passion and confidence to study.

音樂是相當撫慰人心的。念書時聽柔性音樂是我學術成功的關鍵，**而這想法來自於英語教學理論中的暗示性教學。我實際上將這個方式改編成另一個形式。聽外國音樂加速我適應其他語言環境的步調。**其他外國語言的音樂就在我心中迴響著，而且我不費吹灰之力就通過了法文和俄羅斯文課程。我想學習中最重要的是首先要知道你的學習型態，你就可以很快掌握其中的韻律而且有足夠的熱情和信心學習。

PART 01 個人喜好

PART 02 二選一話題

PART 03 概述觀點

PART 04 整合文章和講座

PART 05 討論解決辦法

PART 06 概括講座內容

❸ exercising+strict daily routine and structure it

Exercising is the key. I set a strict daily routine for me to study and I structure it. I always do the morning jogging while listening to recorded English course content, and right after the jogging I study history and literature. **Since exercising releases endorphins, I won't have a bad mood studying history and literature, and I pick up lots of vocabularies during morning jogging.** I just need to review them before the test. And I do go to the gym at 8 p.m. Right after I go to the gym and shower, I do several math questions and study physics. Some of my classmates wonder how that's going to work, but misunderstanding exercising can waste your study time can cost an arm and a leg, especially when SAT test day is approaching.

運動是關鍵。我制定了嚴格的日規劃行程來學習並組織它。我總是在做晨間慢跑時聽錄製的英語課程內容，而在慢跑後我研讀歷史和文學。**既然運動釋放了腦內啡，我不會在讀歷史和文學時有壞心情，而且我在晨間慢跑時，掌握許多字彙。**我僅需要在考試前複習一下子。而且我在晚間八點會去健身房。我去健身房和淋浴後，我會做幾道數學題和研讀物理。我有些同學會想這怎麼能運作，**但是誤解運動會浪費你的學習時間會付出極大代價，特別是當SAT考試即將到來的時候。**

解析

第一個回答包含了使用不同學科和學習方式有何特性去回答這個話題，讓考官很能去連結，考官也會想到自己當初學這個科目的過程，而你提出的看法有什麼不同，最後講述自己本身為何因此受惠和提出看法，是個活潑的答法。

第二個回答在活潑中融入的實際體驗，還提到暗示性教學法和因此不費吹灰之力就通過了法文和俄羅斯文課程，還有學習型態的重要性，是個讓考官一聽就會喜歡的答法。

最後一個答法講到運動是關鍵。最棒的是有融入個人經驗和時間的分配，結尾更幽默的表達出，特別是當SAT考試即將到來的時候，讓個人經驗描述更為真實，不像是硬掰的答案。這三個答案都很值得參考喔！

PART 01　個人喜好

PART 02　二選一話題

PART 03　概述觀點

PART 04　整合文章和講座

PART 05　討論解決辦法

PART 06　概括講座內容

交通
工作、生活或旅遊中所偏好的交通工具

Narrator: You will now be asked a question about a familiar topic. After you read the question, you will have 15 seconds to prepare your response and 45 seconds to speak.

Task 1 "Describe the most enjoyable transportation. Use specific examples and details to support your opinion."
▶ **MP3 007**

口說 回答

請先別看後面的參考答案，自己練習一次，看自己聽到問題會如何回答這題，練習過後，可以參考書中三個回答，並將佳句記下和觀看解析，用於應考中，更無往不利。

_____

_____

_____

_____

_____

_____

_____

_____

_____

_____

(Prepare time: 15 seconds，Response time: 45 seconds)

01 PART 個人喜好

02 PART 二選一話題

03 PART 概述觀點

04 PART 整合文章和講座

05 PART 討論解決辦法

06 PART 概括講座內容

❶ Trains

Trains of course. Taking a train makes you relaxed during the journey of the trip, and **you get to see all the beautiful scenery passing by in swift review.** In addition, you have plenty of time to do your own thing. **Things have always been hectic with work and love life and so on…sitting on the train, you eventually have a little time to reflect on things happening lately** to see if there is anything you did wrong or to figure out how to avoid an embarrassing situation. Plus, sometimes an idea pops out of nowhere…it's amazing actually.

當然是火車啊!旅程途中期間搭火車讓你感到放鬆,而且美麗的景色很快速地映入眼簾。此外,你有許多時間做自己要做的事。總是因為工作和感情生活等等的事感到忙亂…坐在火車內,你最終有點時間去思考最近所發生的事情,看是否你有做錯的或了解如何避免一場令人感到尷尬的情況。再者,有時候一個想法不知道從哪蹦出…這著實令人感到吃驚。

❷ Bicycles

I would definitely choose the bicycle. The enjoyment of taking a bicycle is beyond anything. **Exercising pacifies your mind and burns extra calories.** In addition, exercising eases your stress and it is especially helpful when you take a bike to work. **Even though you have to like go an extraordinary length to take an extra suit to work and change it, you can totally feel like Sandra Bullock in the Proposal.** The benefits of the morning exercise is just beyond description. Of course, you have to experience it to realize that it's true. I guess people might change their perception and choose bicycling, too.

我確定會選擇腳踏車。搭乘腳踏車的享受超過任何事情。運動緩和心智而且燃燒額外的卡路里。此外，運動舒緩你的壓力而且對於騎乘腳踏車上班的人來說特別有幫助。即使你必須要大費周張攜帶額外的套裝到工作場合並做更換，你可以全然感到像是在「愛情限時簽」電影中珊卓布拉克那樣。晨間運動的益處超乎所能想像的。當然，你必須要經歷後才能體會到它的真實性。我想人們可能會改變他們的觀點，也改選擇腳踏車呢？

PART 01 個人喜好

PART 02 二選一話題

PART 03 概述觀點

PART 04 整合文章和講座

PART 05 討論解決辦法

PART 06 概括講座內容

❸ Automobiles

Are you kidding me? Of course, the automobile. **You can feel the breeze coming from all the bystanders when you are driving. The polished windshield and the car totally represent the kind of the person a car driver himself.** I'm not going to brag about the car I'm driving, but I do enjoy being the center of the attention. And driving the automobile just gives me exactly that. In addition, seeing other colleagues driving motorcycles to work during the rainy day is just so painful to watch. They might catch a cold even with the raincoat on. I do hope one day they will enjoy the benefit of driving the automobile as I do.

　　你在開玩笑嗎？當然是汽車啊！當你開車時，你可以感覺到一股微風從旁觀者那頭吹過來。光鮮亮麗的擋風玻璃和車子全然可以代表著汽車駕駛本身。我不是要吹牛自己所駕駛的車子，但是我會喜愛成為關注的焦點。而且駕駛汽車給我那樣的感覺。此外，看到其他同事們在雨天時騎乘摩托車，很慘不忍睹。他們即使穿著雨衣也可能會感冒。我很希望有天他們能夠跟我一樣享受駕駛汽車的好處。

🔑 解析

　　這個題目主要的是要先選定一個交通工具，然後腦海中要有構想和特色，才能接續講到時間結束。第一個回答提到坐火車的優點，並融入了生活體驗，最後很輕鬆的結尾。

　　第二個回答也提到了搭乘腳踏車的好處，especially helpful和go an extraordinary length都讓語氣表達更自然，然後是提到you can totally feel like Sandra Bullock in the Proposal，能讓考官覺得幽默又會心一笑的感覺，好像聽了很多制式回答，突然聽到蠻生動的答案的感覺。提到電影和明星等更能拉近跟考官的距離，最後以疑問句結尾也很棒。

　　第三個答案是以問句開頭，先提問再表達自己的看法。然後提到汽車的優點和為什麼選擇汽車。Gives me exactly that等表達都讓同事覺得更像是口說對談，最後提到自己看到同事雨天騎車的感觸。考生可以看完這三個回答後，想想自己會選哪個交通工具，並將答案列出自己也練習下吧！

PART 01 個人喜好

PART 02 二選一話題

PART 03 概述觀點

PART 04 整合文章和講座

PART 05 討論解決辦法

PART 06 概括講座內容

個人規劃
描述對未來的目標
（存第一桶金：一百萬美元、替野生動物募款和創業）

Narrator: You will now be asked a question about a familiar topic. After you read the question, you will have 15 seconds to prepare your response and 45 seconds to speak.

Task 1 Your Own Goal
Describe your future goal. Use specific examples and details to support your opinion .

▶ **MP3 009**

回說 回答

請先別看後面的參考答案，自己練習一次，看自己聽到問題會如何回答這題，練習過後，可以參考書中三個回答，並將佳句記下和觀看解析，用於應考中，更無往不利。

_____

_____

_____

_____

_____

_____

_____

_____

_____

_____

(Prepare time: 15 seconds，Response time: 45 seconds)

PART 01 個人喜好

PART 02 二選一話題

PART 03 概述觀點

PART 04 整合文章和講座

PART 05 討論解決辦法

PART 06 概括講座內容

 ▶MP3 010

❶ A million US dollars

My goal is to save a million US dollars. In Taiwan, you can frequently hear people's goal in life is to save a million NT dollars. Mine is to save a million US dollars, which is about 30 times that of most people. But why not? You have to dream big…sort of like Judy Hops from Zootopia. When she is given the task by the Chief that she should write a hundred tickets a day. She set the goal of writing two hundred on the first day at work. To me, dreaming big is very important, and the money saved has a total say in your later life, and how quick you reach that point will determine how successful you are in your later life, according to some studies…so a million US dollars here I come.

　　我的目標是存一百萬美元。在台灣，你可以常聽到人們的人生的目標是存一百萬台幣。我的話則是存一百萬美元，也就是大概大多數人目標的30倍左右。但是為何不呢？你必須要將夢做大…有點像是動物方程式電影裡的朱蒂‧哈普斯。當她知道警長要她的第一個任務是開一百張罰單，她定了第一天上工要開兩百張罰單的目標。對我而言，將夢想做大很重要，而且所存的金錢對於你往後的生活有著絕對的決定權，還有你多快達到那個目標會決定你往後生或能有多成功，根據有些研究…所以一百萬美元我來了。

❷ Raising money for wild animals

My goal is to raise money for wild animals. It seems kind of different from the goal everyone would do, but it's meaningful and unique in my eye⋯ kind of like the concept in Adam Braun's *The Promise of the Pencil*⋯.the only difference is I focus on the wild animals. Some wild animals live a tortured life that is just so unbearable. **Elephants get beaten to death and sloth bears get eaten.** People need to understand that a small change in the ecosystem will eventually have a drastic effect on the place where we live. Raising money for them will turn their lives around and hopefully raise the awareness of hardships of wild animals.

　　我的目標是替野生動物募款。這似乎會與每個人會想要定的目標有所不同，但是在我眼中這是很有意義且獨特的⋯有點像是亞當・巴塱的「鉛筆的希望」⋯唯一個差異在於我是聚焦在野生動物身上。有些野生動物過著飽受折磨的生活，令人看了難以忍受。**大象被鞭打致死而懶熊被食用。** 人們需要了解到生態系統中很小的一個改變最終會對於我們所居住的地方有著急遽的影響。替它們募款最終扭轉它們的生活而且希望能喚起對於野生動物所處困境的意識。

PART 01 個人喜好

PART 02 二選一話題

PART 03 概述觀點

PART 04 整合文章和講座

PART 05 討論解決辦法

PART 06 概括講座內容

❸ Start my own company

My answer is to start my own company. **You don't need to have an MBA to know that a fixed income won't get you anywhere.** And in life, we all have lots of things we would like to do. Starting your own company will not only help you realize your dream, but also help you stay out of the comfort zone. Once you start your own company and do things you are passionate about, you have to put 100% of you in the business you are in, and there is no turning back. **You won't be the kind of the person who sits comfortably in the office counting the holiday, and then out of the blue is made redundant to the boss.**

我的答案是開創我自己的公司。你不需要有**MBA**才知道固定薪水並不能讓你一展所長。而且在生活中，我們都有許多事情是我們想從事的。開創你自己的公司不僅僅是能幫助你實現你自己的夢想，而且也能幫助你脫離舒適圈。一旦你開創了你自己的公司和從事你所感到熱忱的事情，你必須要付出**100%**的努力在你的事業上，而且沒有回頭路。你不會像是坐在辦公室裡頭數著假期的人那般，而且突然間對於老闆來說是多餘的。

🔑 解析

　　這題的話其實跟我們更息息相關，除了思考答案外，也能想想自己最近所設立的目標並表達出來。第一個答案很有特色，存第一桶金，但卻是超越版的，因為是存一百萬美元，還融入了動物方城市的內容，讓人感覺活潑和有自己的想法，最後還說了「…所以一百萬美元我來了」，只能說這是超高分口說答案了。

　　第二個答案是很遠大的夢想，然後融入了一本蠻值得看的書籍*The Promise of the Pencil*，最後拉回自己本身，且用最近的新聞來解釋，全然像個想法獨特且具思考性的學習者，是個令人印象深刻的回答。

　　最後一個答案是開創自己的公司，是個很實用性的回答，還提到了then out of the blue is made redundant to the boss.，哈哈，希望我們都不要遇到這樣的情況XDD。

PART 01 個人喜好

PART 02 二選一話題

PART 03 概述觀點

PART 04 整合文章和講座

PART 05 討論解決辦法

PART 06 概括講座內容

個人特質
描述對一個人來說最重要的特質

Narrator: You will now be asked a question about a familiar topic. After you read the question, you will have 15 seconds to prepare your response and 45 seconds to speak.

Task 1 "Describe the most important quality for a person."
▶ **MP3 011**

回說 回答

請先別看後面的參考答案，自己練習一次，看自己聽到問題會如何回答這題，練習過後，可以參考書中三個回答，並將佳句記下和觀看解析，用於應考中，更無往不利。

(Prepare time: 15 seconds，Response time: 45 seconds)

PART 01 個人喜好

PART 02 二選一話題

PART 03 概述觀點

PART 04 整合文章和講座

PART 05 討論解決辦法

PART 06 概括講座內容

❶ Persistence

The most important quality is persistence not because it's something that we are frequently heard like "see persistence pays off in the end" but because "nothing in the world can take the place of persistence." The latter is actually from Ray Kroc's *Grinding It Out,* and how he gets where he is today and how his story inspires many people. Persistence makes him the person he's been known today. **Talent, genius, and education won't take the place of persistence. So be persistent so that you will not give up when mounting pressure or whatever instabilities come to you.**

　　最重要的特質是毅力，不是因為有些我們常聽到話語像是「看吧!最終毅力讓結果有所回報」，而是因為「在這世界上沒有任何事物能取代毅力」。後者實際上是源自於雷・克洛克的「永不放棄：我如何打造麥當勞王國」，而且他如何贏得現今所有的成就和他的故事激勵許多人。毅力成就了我們現今所知道聞名的雷・克洛克。才能、天賦和教育都不能取代毅力的地位。所以保有毅力這樣你才能在壓力排山倒海而來時或者是事情出現任何變動時，抱持不放棄的態度。

❷ highly motivated

The most important quality is to be highly motivated. Remember that's the criteria that HR people use to assess a person's ability in the workplace. it's not just your intelligence or your ability. **It's your motivation to the job and your ability. You multiply one's motivation and one's ability, and then you get what a person will bring to the company.** That's what an employer cares about and you can see what an important role motivation plays in it. A highly motivated person will eventually outperform those who rest on their intelligence and diploma, but with a little motivation. So equip yourself with a highly-motivated mindset.

最重要的特質是有高度動機。記得人事部的人在評估一個人在工作場所能力的標準嗎？不僅僅是你的智力或你的能力。是關於你對於這份工作的動機和你的能力。你將一個人的動機乘上一個人的能力，然後你就可以得知這個人會替公司帶來什麼效益。這是雇主所在乎的而且你可以看到動機在這件事上頭扮演著多重要的角色。具高度動機的人最終會表現超越那些僅仰賴自己本身智力和學歷但卻有著些許動機者。所以將自己包裝能具有高度動機心態者。

PART 01 個人喜好

PART 02 二選一話題

PART 03 概述觀點

PART 04 整合文章和講座

PART 05 討論解決辦法

PART 06 概括講座內容

❸ hard-working

Hard-working is the most important quality for a university student, if he or she wants to be successful. **People with a hedonistic mindset show a less focused attention on the job.** Although we can't guarantee a success if we work hard, we still need to work hard. Often hard-working gradually makes up for the gap between the person who doesn't work hard. One can't expect success, if the person does not work hard. It's the basis in life, and one's achievement lies in hard-working. **The earlier university students understand the value of hard-working, the earlier they can enjoy the success that comes with it.**

努力工作對於一個大學學生來說是最重要的特質，如果他或她想要成功的話。**抱持著享樂主義者展現在工作時展現得較不專注。**儘管我們努力，我們無法保證成功，我們仍需要努力工作。通常努力工作會逐漸補足與不努力工作者間的差距。一個人不能期望著成功，如果這個人不努力工作。這是生命中的基礎，而且一個人的成就取得是在於努力。**大學學生越早了解努力的價值，他們能越早享受隨之而來的成功。**

解析

　　這題很令人省思呢，描述對一個人來說最重要的特質，所以在你心中最重要的特質是什麼呢?可以先想想在看答案。第一個回答很棒，還提到了雷·克洛克的「永不放棄：我如何打造麥當勞王國」輔助說明自己所選的特質為什麼重要，是個聰明的表達方式，而且他影響力很深遠，毅力確實是個很重要的特質，快把這個答案抄下吧XDD。

　　第二個答案有針對答案作出了解釋，蠻實際的回答。此外，還提到了動機乘上能力的部分，並進一步解釋為什麼這個特質會是最重要的，蠻讓人深省的。

　　最後一個回答是提到努力工作的部分。比較會是我們常聽到的老生常談，人要努力，進一步說明努力所能補足本身天賦不足的部分，是個平穩的回答。考生可以三個答案都看一下，也想想自己會怎麼答這題。

PART 01 個人喜好

PART 02 二選一話題

PART 03 概述觀點

PART 04 整合文章和講座

PART 05 討論解決辦法

PART 06 概括講座內容

Narrator: You will now be asked a question about a familiar topic. After you read the question, you will have 15 seconds to prepare your response and 45 seconds to speak.

Task 1 Talk about a famous author that you admire. Use specific examples and details to support your opinion.
▶ **MP3 013**

🗣 口說 回答

請先別看後面的參考答案，自己練習一次，看自己聽到問題會如何回答這題，練習過後，可以參考書中三個回答，並將佳句記下和觀看解析，用於應考中，更無往不利。

_____

_____

_____

_____

_____

_____

_____

_____

_____

(Prepare time: 15 seconds，Response time: 45 seconds)

PART 01 個人喜好

PART 02 二選一話題

PART 03 概述觀點

PART 04 整合文章和講座

PART 05 討論解決辦法

PART 06 概括講座內容

① Tyra Banks

The famous person that I admire is Tyra Banks. She is a remarkable lady. The show America's Next Top Model is so great. From every season, you get to learn wisdom from this lady, not just modeling advice, but also life experience. Modeling is just a part of our life, and life is long. In the show, there is always something, perhaps a story or what she says, that can be so meaningful and can encourage so many younger generations. **People are in desperate need of an inner compass because they can be so lost sometimes. Sometimes what she says can actually lead people to think in a certain direction.** Very helpful.

我最欽佩的名人是泰拉‧班克絲。她是個卓越的女士。全美超模是多麼棒的秀。從每季,你可以從這個女士身上學習到智慧,不僅僅是模特兒的建議,還有生活經驗。模特兒僅是我們生活的一部分,而人生卻是漫長的。在節目中,總會有些事情,或許是故事或她說所的話,都可以是很有意義的,而且能鼓勵許多較年輕的世代。人們迫切需要心理內部的指南針,因為他們可能在有些時候感到迷失。有時候她所說的話實際上可以將人們導向以某個特定方向思考。非常有幫助。

❷ Clayton M. Christensen

Clayton M. Christensen, author of *How Will You Measure Your life* is the famous person that I admire. Through his book, you can always find something to learn, like compendium of wisdom that will be quite helpful for every aspect of your life. I love everything he writes about whether it is a book like *How Will You Measure Your life* or books that are business related. No matter how successful you are in life, **there are moments in life that you just can't figure out at the moment, and reading his books will eventually find something that solves the long-term problem.** I don't know…just admire him like someone who likes Jennifer Anniston or Sandra bullock.

克雷頓・克里斯汀生，「你如何衡量你的人生」的作者是我最欽佩的名人。透過他的書籍，你總是可以找到可以學習的東西，像是濃縮版的智慧寶典，對於你生活的每個面向都相當有助益。我喜愛他所寫的每件事，不論是像是「你如何衡量你的人生」的書籍或是與商業類相關的書籍。不論你在生活中有多成功，總有在某個當下你對有些事情無法理出頭緒，而閱讀他的書籍最終要找到解決問題的長遠辦法。我不知道…對他的欽佩可能像有些人喜歡珍妮佛・安妮斯頓或珊卓・布拉克那樣吧。

PART 01 個人喜好

PART 02 二選一話題

PART 03 概述觀點

PART 04 整合文章和講座

PART 05 討論解決辦法

PART 06 概括講座內容

❸ Ray Kroc

Ray Kroc, the person who built the McDonald's empire, is the person I admire. He is an icon with traditional values and wisdom for later generations to learn from. In his memoir, it reveals he envisions McDonald's restaurants will be popular all over the country. He still believes he has the chance to succeed at the age of 52, totally having a millionaire mind. **His success shows there are no age limits when it comes to success.** Persistence and determination will eventually get you there. Some people just give up too quickly. His individual success can definitely be a great impetus for someone who is still struggling. Such a remarkable man.

雷‧克洛克，一位建造麥當勞帝國的人，是我所欽佩的對象。他是指標性人物，有著傳統價值和智慧讓較後面世代們可以從中學習到很多。在他的回憶錄中，揭漏了他構想麥當勞餐廳會於全國流行開來。在他52歲時，他仍相信自己有機會成功，全然有著百萬富翁的心態。**他的成功展示了，當提到成功時，是沒有年紀限制的。**毅力和決心最終會使你達到你想要的。有些人太快放棄了。他的個人成就肯定能替那些仍在掙扎者帶來大幅度的動力。多麼卓越的男人。

解析

　　這題是詢問你談論一位你所欣賞的作家。考生可以想想自己想要描述的人會是誰。第一個回答是泰拉‧班克絲，除了解釋原因外，也講述到「年輕的人迫切需要心理內部的指南針，因為他們可能在有些時候感到迷失。有時候她所說的話實際上可以將人們導向以某個特定方向思考。」，這部分更進一步闡述了為何欽佩這個人物。

　　第二個人物是位暢銷書作者，除了提到書籍外，回答還包含了對生活的助益，最後結尾以比較活潑的方式結束，像是提到兩個影星，讓對談比較不枯燥。

　　最後一個回答是建造麥當勞帝國的人，其實是很鼓舞人心的，成功是沒有年紀限制了，正因為這樣他才能在老年了還能開創這麼成功的事業，這點真令人欽佩，因為在成功的道路上競爭者真的很少，畢竟會堅持下去的人不多。三個答案中的人物，都曾寫過書籍，且除了是作者外都是很具影響力的人。這類的話題，除了可以用在描述所欣賞的作家外，也可以是令自己感到欽佩的名人或偉人，或者是跟人物類相關的話題都可以使用到喔。考生可以舉一反三，將其中某些句子更改後，人物類的話題其實都通用。

PART 01 個人喜好

PART 02 二選一話題

PART 03 概述觀點

PART 04 整合文章和講座

PART 05 討論解決辦法

PART 06 概括講座內容

工作話題
一份未來你所想要從事的工作

Narrator: You will now be asked a question about a familiar topic. After you read the question, you will have 15 seconds to prepare your response and 45 seconds to speak.

Task 1 The special job you would like to do in the future.
▶ **MP3 015**

口說 回答

請先別看後面的參考答案，自己練習一次，看自己聽到問題會如何回答這題，練習過後，可以參考書中三個回答，並將佳句記下和觀看解析，用於應考中，更無往不利。

_____

_____

_____

_____

_____

_____

_____

(Prepare time: 15 seconds，Response time: 45 seconds)

❶ an island guard

The special job I would like to do in the future is the island guard. Those islands are owned by very wealthy people. Places on the island will be decorated like holiday resorts, and I love beach and enjoy sunshine. This motivates a lot simply because every morning when you are awake, you get to see beautiful scenery out there. This is what turns me on. **You just need to do what you love so that you have the impetus to motivate you to wake up.** Some people might say something like you will get bored eventually, but that's just because you see things in a monotonous way. Take trees for example, they are so different in four seasons, and plus there are lots of different things on the island.

　　未來我想要從事的特別工作是島嶼看守員。那些島嶼是由非常富有的人所擁有的。島上的地方會被裝飾成像渡假勝地般，而且我喜愛海灘和享受陽光。這大大地驅策著我因為每個早晨當你醒來，你能夠看到外頭的美麗景色。這就是能讓我感到興奮的點。**你就是需要從事你喜愛的工作，這樣一來你才會有動力驅策你起床。**有些人可能會說像是你最終會對此感到厭倦的，但是這是因為你只以單一個方式看事物。以樹木為例，它們在四季都如此不同，而且再說島上還有很多不同的事物在。

❷ taste tester at a brewery or a chocolate plant

The special job I would like to do in the future is a chocolate eater or a beer drinker. Someone actually pays you to eat or drink. I don't think any job can compete with it. Take eating chocolate for example, you get to eat different kinds and some are decorated with fancy decorations. You can eat them before they are on the market. All you have to do is to fabricate something insightful and your job is done. How easy. And as for the drinking beer, are you kidding, your boss just gives you the permission to drink at work, and you can joke about it when your friends invite you to have a drink, like I think I've had enough during work, and they surprisingly respond to you, oh right…you are a taste tester…how fun…ha

----

在未來我想要從事的特別工作是巧克力或啤酒品嚐員。有人實際上付你錢要你吃或喝東西。我不認為任何工作能與之相比。以巧克力品嚐員為例，你能夠吃各式不同種類的而且有些巧克力還以豪華方式裝飾。你可以在上市前就吃到它們。你所需要做的只是編造一些有洞察力的評論，然後你的工作就完成了。多容易啊!而至於啤酒品嚐員的話，你在開玩笑嗎，你的老闆給你在上班可以喝酒的許可了，而且當你朋友邀請你去喝一杯時，你可以開個玩笑，像是我想我在上班時已經喝夠了，而且他們會令你感到驚訝地回覆你，噢，對了…你是啤酒品嚐員…多好玩啊…哈。

01 個人喜好 PART

02 二選一話題 PART

03 概述觀點 PART

04 整合文章和講座 PART

05 討論解決辦法 PART

06 概括講座內容 PART

❸ cartoon writers

The special job I would like to do in the future is be a cartoon writer. What's more fun than being a cartoon writer? **You fabricate some stories and you're done for the day.** Once in a while, the company sends you to several amazing places for you to study how animals behave so that you can depict certain animals more specifically, and of course audiences love the genuine feelings you describe. **You get to enjoy yourself during all these trips and learn and it boosts your creativity in some ways.** You will get more ideas in some exotic places. You write stories that can be an instant hit. For you and the company. Win-win.

在未來我想要從事的特別工作是卡通寫作者。還能有比當卡通寫作者好玩的工作了嗎？**你編造一些故事，然後你今天就到這為止了。**偶爾，公司會送你到幾個令人感到驚奇的地方去研究下動物如何表現自己，如此一來你就能夠更確切地描繪出特定的動物，而當然觀眾喜愛你所描繪出的真實感。**你可以在這些假期時自我享受一下並學習，而這些都能在某種程度上增進你的創意。**你會在一些異國風情的地方有更多想法。你寫的故事可能會立刻大紅。對你和公司來說。雙贏。

解析

　　這題很能讓考生發揮創意，將自己未來想從事的工作表達出很容易，或是過去有具特色的工作也能憑藉之前的工作經驗而能輕易回答這題。三個回答都具創意且富含特色。第一個是島嶼看守員。除了融入海灘和陽光外，也提到興奮點為何，最後更畫龍點睛地提到四季變化等，是個妙答啊！

　　第二個回答也很活潑，「在上市前就吃到它」和「只是編造一些有洞察力的評論」都讓考官或聽者感受到還真特別或真容易啊，工作真的只要這樣嗎或也太簡單吧，邊聽邊笑一下。「噢，對了…你是啤酒品嚐員…多好玩啊…哈」也讓人覺得不像是背誦答案的輕鬆閒聊，很棒的回答。

　　最後一個答案也蠻不錯的，也融入了這份工作的優點等，這些都是未來為什麼會想從事這份工作的原因，蠻棒的。其實除了對於未來工作的回答外，其實也可以用在關於現在或過去工作的描述上或者是跟工作相關的話題都用使用到喔。回答中的很多佳句都適用於工作類話題，快記下來吧。

PART 01 個人喜好

PART 02 二選一話題

PART 03 概述觀點

PART 04 整合文章和講座

PART 05 討論解決辦法

PART 06 概括講座內容

part 2

二選一
日常話題

二選一日常話題精選了 8 個主題提供考生練習，每個題目也同樣提供考生三個回答作為參考。遇到這類型的題目其實只要馬上決定好兩個選擇中要選擇哪方，並在腦海中浮現幾個關鍵字，該關鍵字能支持你所想要選擇的立場或決定，就能答好這題。可以看下三個回答中如何將答題更自然化，並融入自己的口語語庫中，有的口語句型可能在其他 part 也用的到喔！

金錢、消費習慣和理財
該將額外的錢花掉還是存起來

Narrator: You will now be asked to give your opinion about a familiar topic. After you read the question, you will have 15 seconds to prepare your response and 45 seconds to speak.

Task 2 "Spend the extra money or save it. Which do you prefer?"
▶**MP3 017**

回說 回答

請先別看後面的參考答案，自己練習一次，看自己聽到問題會如何回答這題，練習過後，可以參考書中三個回答，並將佳句記下和觀看解析，用於應考中，更無往不利。

_____

_____

_____

_____

_____

_____

_____

_____

_____

_____

(Prepare time: 15 seconds，Response time: 45 seconds)

PART 01 個人喜好

PART 02 二選一話題

PART 03 概述觀點

PART 04 整合文章和講座

PART 05 討論解決辦法

PART 06 概括講座內容

① Save the extra money

Of course, the answer is to save the extra money. Remember the old wisdom from *The Richest Man in Babylon*, money comes to those who save it. **Frittering away with the money can only give you the transient pleasure, but once the excitement goes away, you are right back to where you are.** A one-time lottery winner can lose lots of money in a short time and be seen living under a bridge of the freezing winter night, let alone the person who earns a fixed income. In addition, you just don't know what life is going to test you. Without the saving, you will regret when something bad happens to you.

當然，答案是存下額外的錢。記得「巴比倫最富有的人」裡頭的古老智慧嗎？，金錢來自於那些將它存下者。**揮霍浪費掉金錢只會使你獲得短暫的樂趣，但是一旦那種興奮感消逝，你馬上回到本來的狀態。**曾經的樂透得主可能在短期間就失去許多錢，然後於寒冷的冬天夜晚被發現在橋下住著，更別說是只賺取固定薪資者。此外，你就是不會知道生命在未來考驗著你什麼。沒有了存款，你會在厄運來臨時後悔莫及。

❷ Save the extra money

Save the extra money. I'm an advocate of living your life to the fullest, and like everyone once in a while I do indulge myself with a little shopping and international trips. But that money is not from my payment, my fixed income. It's from the house rent every month I receive, and you can't spend your fixed income on luxuries and international trips. You can only use your bonuses, investment money from the stock market, or house rent you receive on leisure activities or for pleasure. **So saving money⋯till you have the capability to enjoy the fruit of it.** At that moment, you spend it on something you enjoy.

存下額外的錢。我是主張人該盡其所能享受自己的人生者，而且像每個人一樣偶爾我也會縱容自己有些購物和去國際旅行。但是那些金錢不是來自於我的薪資，我固定的收入。而是來自於每個月我所收到的租金，你就是不能使用你的固定收入花費在奢侈品和國際旅遊上。你可能僅能使用你的獎金、從股市投資賺來的錢、或是你所收到的房租來從事休閒活動或得到樂趣。**所以存錢吧⋯直到你有能力享用存錢後所帶來的果實。**在那時候，你可以花費在一些你喜愛的東西上。

PART 01 個人喜好

PART 02 二選一話題

PART 03 概述觀點

PART 04 整合文章和講座

PART 05 討論解決辦法

PART 06 概括講座內容

❸ spend it right away

Spend it right away…since I'm not planning to have kids, start a family, buy a house, and so on. Why can't I just spend all the extra money…and to be honest, **saving for the rainy day thing is an old concept…you just have to let go of it.** In life, you can't even know what's going to happen to you in the next second. No one knows…even the fortune-teller does not. So I definitely will be the kind of the person who cherishes every moment and enjoys every moment of life…and of course with the EXTRA MONEY.

馬上花掉…既然我不打算要有小孩、成家立業、買房子等等的。為什麼我不能花掉所有額外的金錢呢…**而且說實話，未雨綢繆是老舊的觀點了…你就是該放掉這個觀點。**在生命中，你甚至無法得知下一秒你會發生什麼事。沒有人知道…甚至算命師都不知道。所以我肯定是那種珍惜每個當下的人，而且享受生命中每個時刻…當然附帶著會用掉額外的金錢。

解析

　　這是二選一的回答。三個回答中有兩個是贊成要存下錢，其中一個答案是馬上花掉。第一個包含了俏皮式地詢問記得「巴比倫最富有的人」裡頭的古老智慧嗎？引起聽者興趣和好奇。最後也舉出實例，包含樂透贏家最後將錢花光淪落街頭的事，讓人深省。

　　第二個回答也是贊成要存下錢。實際的表明原因，包含不能使用本薪來買奢侈品等，是個實用的回答，很值得學習。

　　最後一個答案是立即花光錢，比較享樂主義，但也無不可，回答中表達的自然且活潑，其實只要表達出個人看法且英語流暢即可，選擇立即花光也不會影響考官對你的評分，盡情答吧！

PART 01 個人喜好

PART 02 二選一話題

PART 03 概述觀點

PART 04 整合文章和講座

PART 05 討論解決辦法

PART 06 概括講座內容

社交

結交朋友
（喜歡與親密朋友一塊還是與各式各樣的朋友在一起）

Narrator: You will now be asked to give your opinion about a familiar topic. After you read the question, you will have 15 seconds to prepare your response and 45 seconds to speak.

Task 2 "Close friends or a variety of friends. Which do you prefer?"

▶**MP3 019**

口說 回答

請先別看後面的參考答案，自己練習一次，看自己聽到問題會如何回答這題，練習過後，可以參考書中三個回答，並將佳句記下和觀看解析，用於應考中，更無往不利。

_____

_____

_____

_____

_____

_____

_____

_____

_____

(Prepare time: 15 seconds，Response time: 45 seconds)

PART 01 個人喜好

PART 02 二選一話題

PART 03 概述觀點

PART 04 整合文章和講座

PART 05 討論解決辦法

PART 06 概括講座內容

 **一問三答** ▶MP3 020

❶ with close friends

It varies from person to person. **Personality types weigh heavily on this question.** Since I'm a bit of an introvert, I would definitely choose the latter one. **Speaking and hanging out with lots of friends drains your energy quite a bit**, and a shy person like me just doesn't like tons of friends getting together which makes you so burned out. It's my free time, and it's supposed to be like relax and spend some quality time with some of your besties and have drinks. **You don't have to spend so much time engaging in idle gossip, and doing superficial stuff.**

對每個人來說不一樣。個性的類型在這個問題上佔了很重的分配。因為我有點內向，我肯定會想要選後者。說話和與許多朋友閒晃榨乾你相當多的能量，而且像我一樣害羞的人不喜歡有一堆朋友聚在一起，這讓你感到如此筋疲力竭。這是我的空閒時間，而且這應該要像是放鬆而且花些品質時間與一些你的閨密相聚和喝幾杯。你不會需要花費許多時間在聊閒話八卦和做一些表面功夫的東西。

❷ a wide variety of friends and acquaintances

I would love to spend time with a wide variety of friends and acquaintances. You get to learn from different kinds of friends even though you have to do the superficial stuff. You just don't know how sometimes a nodding acquaintance can be quite helpful if you are out there looking for your ideal jobs. **People within your circle; however, often can only have emotional support, but have nothing to offer.** A person I know from the party once introduced me to the industry I've been longing to get into. I eventually get the job even though I have no experiences. **From that moment on, I'm sort of like what the heck, the more the merrier.**

我喜愛把時間花在與各式各樣的朋友和熟識朋友上。你能從不同類型的朋友中學習，即使你必須要做些表面功夫。你不知道有時候就是這樣的點頭之交，在你想要找你的理想工作時發揮相當大的功用。人們自己的圈子裡頭，然而，通常只有著情感支持，但是卻沒什麼能幫上忙的。一位我從派對上認識的人有次引介我進了我一直想要進入的產業裡。我最終獲取工作，即使我沒有經驗。從那個時刻起，我有點像是管它的，越多人越熱鬧。

PART 01 個人喜好

PART 02 二選一話題

PART 03 概述觀點

PART 04 整合文章和講座

PART 05 討論解決辦法

PART 06 概括講座內容

❸ a wide variety of friends and acquaintances

I love my close friends, but sometimes they just bore me in a certain way. Sometimes I want to yell stop already, didn't I just click the like button for your kids' progress in learning the violin. They sometimes just can't give me something in return. With a wide variety of friends, **I can often shift my attention to something novel…like wow you bought yourself a car…or since when…you are raising a chameleon, seriously?** As a Gemini, I do need different kinds of things to make me spirited and keep me intrigued, and thank god I have hundreds of friends…just love the crowd of friends gathering together.

　　我喜愛我的親密朋友，但有時候他們某些程度上只是讓我感到無聊。有時候我想要大叫，快停止啊！我不是才點了你的孩子們學習小提琴進展的「讚」嗎？他們有時候就是無法讓我獲得預期相對的回應。有著各式各樣的朋友時，我通常可以將我的專注力放在一些新奇的事情上…像是哇你替你自己買了一台車嗎…或是是什麼時候的事…你在養變色龍，是真的嗎？身為一個雙子座，我真的需要不同的事物讓我感到有精神或有興趣，而謝天謝地我有上百個朋友…我就是喜愛一群朋友聚在一塊的感覺。

解析

　　這題也是二選一的答題。第一個回答有先解釋個性的類型其實有影響選擇，緊接著提到對內向者來說與人互動消耗能量等等的原因，後面更有engaging in idle gossip等活潑的回答。

　　第二個回答表達也很活潑，且描述到因為與各式朋友相處所帶來的益處，包含進入了另一個產業，最後更俏皮的結尾，像是管它的，越多人越熱鬧，很令人印象深刻。

　　第三個回答也很活潑，像是快停止啊，我不是才點了你的孩子們學習小提琴進展的「讚」嗎？，有點像是抱怨又會讓聽者覺得是閒話家常，後面的回答也非常口語像是「像是哇你替你自己買了一台車嗎...或是是什麼時候的事...你在養變色龍，是真的嗎？」，最後解釋到喜歡一群朋友聚在一塊的感覺完成答題。

PART 01 個人喜好

PART 02 二選一話題

PART 03 概述觀點

PART 04 整合文章和講座

PART 05 討論解決辦法

PART 06 概括講座內容

課堂問題和師生互動

指定座位還是非指定座位

Narrator: You will now be asked to give your opinion about a familiar topic. After you read the question, you will have 15 seconds to prepare your response and 45 seconds to speak.

Task 2 "Often students are more encouraged to participate in the class, if they have the right to choose whatever they like. Which do you prefer? Assigned seats or unassigned seats."

▶MP3 021

回說 回答

請先別看後面的參考答案，自己練習一次，看自己聽到問題會如何回答這題，練習過後，可以參考書中三個回答，並將佳句記下和觀看解析，用於應考中，更無往不利。

_____

_____

_____

_____

_____

_____

_____

_____

_____

(Prepare time: 15 seconds，Response time: 45 seconds)

PART 01 個人喜好

PART 02 二選一話題

PART 03 概述觀點

PART 04 整合文章和講座

PART 05 討論解決辦法

PART 06 概括講座內容

 一問三答 ▶MP3 022

① different seats

Different seats. I do think people who answer students should sit in assigned seats are probably not teachers or they probably haven't seen the movie School of Life. **See what turns out at the end, you will probably rethink about this question.** The assigned seats are fixed and students are feeling so rigid. It's like a traditional setting. Students listen to what the teacher has to say. Often students are more encouraged to participate in the class, if they have the right to choose whatever they like. Plus, I just don't want to feel so awkward all the time.

不同的座位。我確實認為回答學生該座指定位置的人，可能本身不是老師或他們可能沒看過「優良教師爭奪戰」這部電影。**看最後結果是怎樣，你可能就會重新思考這題的問題了。** 指定座位是固定的而學生覺得太嚴格了。這像是傳統教學環境。學生聽老師所要講的話。通常學生更受到鼓勵參與課堂，如果他們有權選擇他們想要的。再者，我就是不想要整個上課時段都感到笨拙。

❷ different seats

Different seats. Assigned seats are just an excuse for teachers to conveniently do the roll call and it does not require any effort to memorize every student. In addition, there are lots of different things that will the students' ability to focus. **I don't want to sit next to a weird person…you know the weird type…I will get so distracted that I can't recall what the teacher said during the whole lecture.** After class, I carry such a negative mood when I go home, and have to work extra hard to keep up with other students…totally a nightmare…

　　不同的座位。指定座位只是能便於老師點名的藉口，而且不需要花費任何努力去記所有學生名字。此外，有許多事情會干擾學生專注力。我不想坐在奇怪的人旁邊…你知道的奇怪類型的人…我會如此分心以至於我沒辦法在整堂課期間回想出老師剛才說了些什麼。在下課後，我回家時會帶著如此負面的情緒在，而且我必須要更努力才能追趕上其他學生…真的是個夢魘…。

❸ assigned seats

Assigned seats. You can develop a strong relationship with the person sitting next to you, if it's assigned seating. **Just don't use that as a way for you to cheat⋯like asking the person you are sitting next to let you peek a little during the test⋯kidding⋯**I don't know I just love assigned seats. Whenever you walk into the classroom, you quickly shift into the mode of oh⋯this is my seat..you don't have to think too much. It's just too tiresome with different seats on different days⋯and having someone telling you that so it's Wednesday so probably you need to move your ass to somewhere else⋯totally makes me mad⋯just give me an assigned seat.

指定座位。如果是指定座位的話，你可以與座你旁邊的人發展出濃厚的關係。只是別將這個方式用來便於自己作弊⋯像是要求座你隔壁的人，在考試時讓你偷看一些些⋯開玩笑的啦⋯我不知道我就是喜愛指定座位。每當你走進教室時，你可以很快地進入模式裡的噢⋯這是我的座位⋯你不用想太多。每天都坐不同的座位讓人感覺太累了⋯而且有個人跟你說今天是星期三，所以你可能需要移至其他地方座⋯整個讓我覺得生氣⋯就給我指定座位就好啦!

解析

　　這題也是二選一的回答。第一個回答提到了「優良教師爭奪戰」這部電影，讓人印象深刻，能引起共鳴，且可以進一步說明為什麼想要選非指定座位的原因，是個巧妙安排的答法，可以偷學起來。

　　第二個回答也讓考官會覺得像是與人對談，而不是背答案，包含了I don't want to sit next to a weird person…you know the weird type…I will get so distracted that和…totally a nightmare…，像是學生間的聊天。

　　最後一個是回答指定座位。當中融入了幽默感，像是Just don't use that as a way for you to cheat…like asking the person you are sitting next to let you peek a little during the test…kidding，還有後面以更口語化的方式講到不同座位讓人生氣的原因，是個很棒的答法。

PART 01 個人喜好

PART 02 二選一話題

PART 03 概述觀點

PART 04 整合文章和講座

PART 05 討論解決辦法

PART 06 概括講座內容

12 生活方式
談論生活模式的改變

Narrator: You will now be asked to give your opinion about a familiar topic. After you read the question, you will have 15 seconds to prepare your response and 45 seconds to speak.

Task 2 Talk about changes in lifestyles
▶ **MP3 023**

回說 回答

請先別看後面的參考答案，自己練習一次，看自己聽到問題會如何回答這題，練習過後，可以參考書中三個回答，並將佳句記下和觀看解析，用於應考中，更無往不利。

_____

_____

_____

_____

_____

_____

_____

_____

_____

_____

(Prepare time: 15 seconds，Response time: 45 seconds)

PART 01 個人喜好

PART 02 二選一話題

PART 03 概述觀點

PART 04 整合文章和講座

PART 05 討論解決辦法

PART 06 概括講座內容

❶

People nowadays have bombarded messages from TVs, Videos on platforms, such as You tube and Facebook. Whether those messages are having what we call marketing thing involved, people are able to learn how to lead a healthy life from watching them. TV programs invite doctors and health specialists educating people how to eat healthy. News reports inform us of repercussions of eating in a certain way, and people who watch news reports about chronic illnesses and cancers are the result of unhealthy lifestyles **will deep down have a warning label inside to not choose unhealthy foods.** These channels are what people in the past didn't have.

　　人們現今從電視、平台上的視頻，例如youtube和臉書，有著轟炸式的訊息。不論這些訊息是我們所稱的牽涉到行銷，人們能夠從觀看視頻學習如何過著健康的生活。電視節目邀請醫生和健康專家教育人們如何吃的健康。新聞報導告知我們以特定方式的飲食習慣會帶來的後果，而且人們觀看關於慢性病和癌症的新聞報導是不健康的生活型態的結果，**這將在內心深處有著警告的標誌留下，提醒你別選擇不健康的食物。**這些頻道是人們過去所沒有的。

❷

People nowadays have so many options in life and they tend to make a comparison with others, whether it is the figures or appearances. They have current technologies to help them get there. They go to the gyms at the specific hours to keep them from being couch potatoes or having sedentary lifestyles. They want to look good on the outside so that they calculate every calorie they consume. **Girls eat only vegetables and fruits with less sugars at night. They do the mini plastics to remove fats in their body.** To keep slim figures for the long-term, having healthy lifestyles is a must. People in the past won't go insanely on this one. They simply content on who they are and what they have inherited from their parents.

　　人們現今在生活中有許多選擇而他們傾向與他人做比較，不論是在體態或外表上。他們有著現今的科技幫助他們達到結果。他們在特定的時候去健身房，使自己免於成為沙發上的馬鈴薯或有著久坐不動的生活型態。他們想要在外在上看起來好看，所以他們就會計算每項他們所攝取的卡路里。**女孩在晚間只吃蔬菜和糖分較少的水果。他們作微整形手術移除他們體內的脂肪。**為了長期維持苗條的身材，有健康的生活型態是必須的。人們在過去不會在這個面向上這麼瘋狂。他們會滿足於他們是怎樣的人還有他們從父母身上得到的遺傳特質。

PART 01 個人喜好

PART 02 二選一話題

PART 03 概述觀點

PART 04 整合文章和講座

PART 05 討論解決辦法

PART 06 概括講座內容

What about people who live on islands or in remote areas? They have healthy lifestyles, and many of them are living to the age of 90 or above. They don't have so many food options, foods that are too exquisite or ones that can easily lead to chronic illness. People nowadays have too many options, and people have a hedonistic mindset. **They think they deserve a little treat to enjoy gourmet once in a while and that leads to unhealthy eating habits and cholesterol blocked blood vessels.** When you have less food and entertainment options, everything becomes simple, and of course leads to a longer lifespan.

那麼關於那些住在島上或邀遠地區的人呢？他們有著健康的生活型態而且他們之中許多人都活到九十歲或更久。他們沒有那麼多樣的食物選擇，太精緻或萃取過的食物，會容易導致慢性病。人們現今有許多選擇，而人們有享樂的心態。他們認為他們值得一些難得的樂事，偶爾享用美食，而這些都導致不健康的飲食習慣和膽固醇堵塞血管。當你對於食物和娛樂有著較少的選擇時，每件事都變得簡單了，而理所當然的有著較長的壽命。

解析

　　這題描述生活方式的改變，其實可以從很多面向去切入，或是用現在的生活模式和過去做比較。也可以與未來期待的生活方式做比較，用差異性襯托出一些想法，這些都影響著我們。第一個回答中提到了轟炸式訊息、電視節目和新聞報導，很實際的表明同意的原因。

　　第二個回答提到人生中的選擇和與他人間的比較等等，論述頗有道理，漸進表達出同意的原因，後面還提到沙發上的馬鈴薯和微整形手術等讓表達更生活化。

　　最後一個答案是先提出疑問，再進一步解釋為何不同意，先題到精緻化的飲食，然後提到慢性病和享樂主義等，最後提到生活簡單化也影響著人是否能健康生活著。除了這三個答案外，考生也可以想想遇到這類話題自己想要說些什麼喔。

PART 01 個人喜好

PART 02 二選一話題

PART 03 概述觀點

PART 04 整合文章和講座

PART 05 討論解決辦法

PART 06 概括講座內容

Narrator: You will now be asked to give your opinion about a familiar topic. After you read the question, you will have 15 seconds to prepare your response and 45 seconds to speak.

Task 2 "Large grocery stores and department stores or small specialty stores. Which do you prefer? "
▶MP3 025

口說 回答

請先別看後面的參考答案，自己練習一次，看自己聽到問題會如何回答這題，練習過後，可以參考書中三個回答，並將佳句記下和觀看解析，用於應考中，更無往不利。

_____

_____

_____

_____

_____

_____

_____

_____

_____

(Prepare time: 15 seconds，Response time: 45 seconds)

PART 01 個人喜好
PART 02 二選一話題
PART 03 概述觀點
PART 04 整合文章和講座
PART 05 討論解決辦法
PART 06 概括講座內容

 ▶MP3 026

❶ large grocery stores and department stores

Definitely large grocery stores and department stores. I just want the feeling of an array of goods and merchandise when I walk into a store. **So pleasing to the eyes. It's like the wow moment**, and they have this and that…you can discuss those things with your friends, and **the excitement of being in a large department stores last like forever**…till you finish your shopping and arrive at home. On-line shopping and small specialty stores just can't give you that kind of enjoyment…and I can't figure out why…I can't tolerate any of my friends who drag me to small specialty stores for shopping. I guess one person being in the store would be too crowded…

當然是大型的食品雜貨店和百貨公司。我就是想要當我走進店裡時，數列貨物和商品陳列的感覺。也太賞心悅目。這就像是「哇」時刻，而且它們有這個和那個…你可以與你的朋友們討論那些商品，而且在大型百貨公司的興奮感像是永久持續般…直到你完成了你的購物和抵達家裡。線上購物和小型特色用品店就是無法給你那樣的喜愛感…而且我也不知道為什麼…我不能忍受我的朋友拉我到小型特色用品店購物。我想一個人置身其中都嫌太擠吧!...。

❷ large grocery stores and department stores

Definitely large grocery stores and department stores. Of course, there are too many options, but you really need to take an in-depth look into everything you buy. After all it is your money that you spend, right? Plus, money is hard to earn. You have to choose something that is really suitable for your need. I can't believe some people **don't even look at the manufacturing dates and put all the groceries in the shopping cart**, and only to regret later on that it has unhealthy contents in there, or the news has warned customers before. Sometimes all you need is just a little bit of patience. You won't spend so much time after previous thorough examinations and comparisons. After shopping several times, you recognize products of every brand and know which brand of milk you would choose and many other items.

當然是大型的食品雜貨店和百貨公司。當然，那裡有許多選擇，但是你真的需要深入了解每項你購買的東西。畢竟是用你的錢買的，對吧？再說，錢很難賺。你必須選擇一些對你來說真的符合需求的東西。我不相信有些人**不用看製造日期就能放整個貨品到購物車裡**，然後於稍後後悔購買的東西有不健康成分在裡頭，或是新聞稍早有警告過消費者過。有時候你所需要的只是一些些耐心。你不用花費那麼多時間在全盤的檢視和比較上。在幾次購物後，你認識了每個品牌的產品而且知道哪個品牌的牛奶是你會選擇的和許多其他項目。

PART 01 個人喜好

PART 02 二選一話題

PART 03 概述觀點

PART 04 整合文章和講座

PART 05 討論解決辦法

PART 06 概括講座內容

❸ small specialty stores

My answer is small specialty stores. Have you heard from what psychologists say that too many options make it harder for people to choose what to buy, and I have to agree with them on this one⋯being in large grocery stores and department stores might be fancy and include thousands of goods, but for some reason, you can't make a decision about which brand is much better. **They all look equally good, and often it takes much longer to finish shopping.** Often my kids and my husband are not happy about it⋯like just pick one⋯ok⋯we are waiting⋯ eventually everyone goes home with a unhappy mood and like it's all my fault. From that moment on, I would prefer small specialty stores.

　　我的答案是小型特色用品店。你有聽過心理學家稱的太多選擇會使人更難對於所要購買的東西做出選擇嗎？而且我必須在這個論述中同意心理學家們所說的⋯置身在大型的食品雜貨店和百貨公司可能感覺奢華和包含上千種商品，但是基於某些理由，你不可能對於哪個品牌較好做出選擇。**它們看起來都相當好，而且通常要花費更長的時間在購物上。** 通常小孩們和我的先生都對此感到不開心⋯像是就選個就好⋯可以嗎？⋯我們在等了⋯最終大家回到家裡有著不愉快的心情，像是都是我的錯一樣。從那時候起，我就會情願在小型特色用品店購物了。

解析

　　這題也是關於論述做出二選一。第一個回答中融入的活潑的答法，包含這就像是「哇」時刻，其後進一步描述興奮的感受，最後更以幽默且反諷的方式講出小型特色用品店的不夠看，真的是妙答啊！

　　第二個的回答蠻實際的，而且有考量到錢難賺等話，語氣跟字句都很流暢，包含and only to regret later on that it has unhealthy contents in there…等等的，可以將這些句型都學習起來用在其他話題中喔！

　　第三個回答則融入了心理學家的看法，讓論點更具有根據性，後面更進一步闡述過多選擇對人行為的影響，是讓人印象深刻的論述。最後以自身經驗強化聽者的感受，差異性比較出所以自己為什麼會選擇喜歡小型特色用品店購物。

PART 01 個人喜好

PART 02 二選一話題

PART 03 概述觀點

PART 04 整合文章和講座

PART 05 討論解決辦法

PART 06 概括講座內容

Narrator: You will now be asked to give your opinion about a familiar topic. After you read the question, you will have 15 seconds to prepare your response and 45 seconds to speak.

Task 2 "Living in a big city or suburban area. Which do you prefer?"
▶ **MP3 027**

🗣 **回說 回答**

請先別看後面的參考答案，自己練習一次，看自己聽到問題會如何回答這題，練習過後，可以參考書中三個回答，並將佳句記下和觀看解析，用於應考中，更無往不利。

_____

_____

_____

_____

_____

_____

_____

_____

_____

_____

_____

(Prepare time: 15 seconds，Response time: 45 seconds)

PART 01 個人喜好

PART 02 二選一話題

PART 03 概述觀點

PART 04 整合文章和講座

PART 05 討論解決辦法

PART 06 概括講座內容

❶ a big city

I do think living in a big city is much better. **Job opportunities abound in big cities.** That's why there is always a gap between the number of people living in the city and the number of people living in the suburban towns. Apart from some elderlies, people need the job to support themselves. Plus, convenience. Living in the city is more convenient. You walk three blocks on the street, and there are an MRT station and U-bikes. The commute time for you from your home to the office is probably only twenty minutes. In addition, there are hundreds of shops in the city. You can buy foods from large grocery stores and often at a cheaper price, and lots of stores open 24/7. Very convenient.

我認為住在大城市裡較好。**在大城市裡頭工作機會充足。** 這就是為什麼住在城市裡的人數和住在郊區小鎮裡的人數總是有差距。除了一些年長者外，人們需要工作來支持生活所需。再者，方便。住在城市裡頭比較方便。你在街上走三個街區，然後那裡就有捷運站和U-bike。從你家到辦公室的通勤時間可能只要花費20分鐘左右。此外，在城市裡頭有數百個店面。你可以從大型百貨公司裡頭購得食物，通常以較便宜的價格購得，而且有許多店是24小時都營業。非常便利。

❷ a big city

I do think living in a big city is much better. It's all about safety. Living in the big city makes you feel safe, and there are several police stations around. You don't have to worry about there being a home invasion…I'm not being paranoid. It happens all the time. Home invasions often occur in the countryside, and in Taiwan you are not allowed to have a gun in your home to protect yourself. **Setting an alarm system seems of little or no use. Most important of all, surveillance cameras are just decorations. When there is a robbery, policemen can't possibly gather any evidence because they usually find out that the surveillance cameras in the countryside are broken.** How awful.

我認為居住在大城市較好。都是與安全性有關。居住在大城市使你感到安全，而且附近會有幾個警察局在。你不用擔心會有人入侵住宅…我不是患有妄想症。這總是發生。住宅入侵的事情通常在鄉村地區常發生，而在台灣你不被允許在家裡擁有槍枝來保護你自己。裝配警報系統幾乎沒有效果。最重要的是，監視器僅是裝飾品。當有搶劫發生時，警察們無法收集任何證據因為他們通常發現在郊區的監視器毀壞了。多麼糟糕啊！

❸ a countryside

Definitely the countryside. I'm not having a second thought about this question. I just don't want to have another purification of the lung thing again. Imagine how many wastes I unconsciously breath into the lung, and **most of them are lingered into the lung**. Sometimes I do have an allergic reaction when I am in the city, but when I am in the countryside I don't have any. Every day it's like breathing into fresh air and you have a pretty good mood about what you are doing. You won't have to find out one day when you are doing the usual routine and then boom···lung disease or other chronic illnesses. I can't imagine any of those panic.

對於這個問題我絲毫沒有任何猶豫。當然鄉村地區囉。我不想要再次地清潔一次我的肺。想像一下有多少的廢棄物，我無意識下吸進肺部，而且**大多數廢棄物質留在肺裡頭**。當我在城市的時候我還會有過敏反應，但是當我在郊區時我不會有任何過敏反應。每天像是吸入新鮮空氣一樣而且你有著相當好的心情做著你正在做的事。你不會有天發現你做著平常習以為常的例行事務然後突然間···轟···肺部疾病和其他慢性疾病跑出來。我就是無法想像任何像那樣子的驚嚇。

解析

　　這題也是屬於二選一的話題。第一個回答是以實際考量為出發點進行論述，有表達出工作在城市裡較好找，並進行列舉，最後更題到便利性，是個平穩的答題。

　　第二個回答是提到安全性，更活潑的表達出「我不是患有妄想症」，之後更題出更多的論述，論點環環相扣，最後指出監視器等問題，論述相當完整，是個很值得學起來的妙答。

　　第三個是選擇鄉村地區，論述讓人聽起來蠻有節奏，讓人可以感受出選擇鄉村的原因是有道理的，最後也很生動地結尾。除了這三個回答外，考生也可以融入自己成長背景，例如在鄉下長大，大學求學到了都市，藉由比較兩者特點，選擇其中一個立場喔!

PART 01 個人喜好

PART 02 二選一話題

PART 03 概述觀點

PART 04 整合文章和講座

PART 05 討論解決辦法

PART 06 概括講座內容

科技對生活造成的改變
閱讀紙張印刷品還是選擇電子書

Narrator: You will now be asked to give your opinion about a familiar topic. After you read the question, you will have 15 seconds to prepare your response and 45 seconds to speak.

Task 2 Some people think that printing materials are still the major medium. Others believe that printed materials will be replaced by electronic versions of those materials. Explain why using specific details in your explanation.
▶**MP3 029**

回說 回答

請先別看後面的參考答案，自己練習一次，看自己聽到問題會如何回答這題，練習過後，可以參考書中三個回答，並將佳句記下和觀看解析，用於應考中，更無往不利。

_____

_____

_____

_____

_____

_____

_____

_____

_____

_____

(Prepare time: 15 seconds，Response time: 45 seconds)

PART 01 個人喜好

PART 02 二選一話題

PART 03 概述觀點

PART 04 整合文章和講座

PART 05 討論解決辦法

PART 06 概括講座內容

❶ materials printed on paper

Hello, printing materials are still the major medium. I don't think that they will be replaced by other e-books. Plus, **reading information through the screen causes eyestrain. The blue light harms one's eyes** and that's why a lot of people cannot look at the computer screen and smartphone screen for longer hours. With books and newspapers, you won't have that kind of problems. You are free to read as long as you want. This is the advantage of reading through books and newspapers. I don't think people can argue with me with this one.

嗨，印刷品仍舊是主要的媒介。我不認為它們會被其他電子書取代。再說，**透過螢幕觀看訊息會導致眼睛疲勞。藍光會傷害眼睛**而且這就是為什麼許多人無法於電腦螢幕和智慧型手機螢幕上觀看較長的一段時間。如果是書籍和報紙的話，你就不會有那樣子的問題。你可以想要閱讀多久就閱讀多久。這是透過閱讀書籍和報紙的優點。我不認為人們可以在這點上跟我爭論。

❷ **replaced by electronic versions of those materials**

I do think one day printed materials will be replaced by electronic versions of those materials. They are just not as convenient. They are too heavy. With e-books, you can read them anywhere…as long as you carry your smartphone or other digital device. **You can read it on the train without having a book weighing down your legs or hands.** You click close, and there you go, you get off the train. **You can even bookmark the page you just finished.** It's just a major transformation that people need to get used to it. Think of film, digital cameras, and so on. They have been replaced by smartphones.

我認為有天印刷品會被電子版本的用具取代。這不僅是因為便利性。有了電子書，你可以到哪都能閱讀…只要你攜帶著你的智慧型手機或其他數位裝置。你在火車上閱讀而不用有著一本書壓著你的雙腳或者手需要支撐書。你點下關閉，然後你就可以結束閱讀、下火車。你甚至可以標籤你剛看完的頁面。這就是主要的改變，而人們就是需要適應它。電影、數位相機等等的，而它們都被智慧型手機取代了呢！

❸ replaced by electronic versions of those materials

I do think one day printed materials will be replaced by electronic versions of those materials. I don't understand why people so fixate on books can't just think outside of the box. It's the trend, and even if reading things through digital devices can cause eyestrain, there are eyeglasses that can significantly reduce the effects blue light has on our eyes, ok? I always wear that kind of glasses so that I won't have any eyestrain, and there are foods and vitamins that can protect you from those problems. Plus, it's more convenient…period.

　　我認為有天印刷品會被電子版本的用具取代。我不能理解為什麼執著於書的人，就是不能跳脫框架思考呢？這是趨勢，而且即使透過數位裝置閱讀會造成眼睛疲勞，有眼鏡能降低藍光對我們眼睛的影響，是吧？我總是帶著那樣子的眼鏡，這樣一來我就不會感到眼睛疲勞了，而且食物和維他命能保護你免於那些問題。再說，這較便利…句點。

解析

　　這題也是二選一的答題。第一個回答有提到實際的原因，包含眼睛疲勞和藍光很傷眼睛等，是個很好的回答開端。之後進一步說了藍光使人們無法於螢幕上觀看較久，這點使得印刷品不會被取代。

　　第二個回答提到了便利性，更活潑地以在火車上閱讀需要用雙腳或手支撐的缺點，輔以使用電子書的便利性做出對照，讓人印象深刻。最後加上了電影和數位相機，感覺又補了一腳，讓聽者或考官更覺得，真是如此，是個很convincing的回答，快偷偷學起來吧!

　　第三個回答是先題到這是趨勢，而且題到藍光眼鏡，表達出還是有產品使讀者能長時間閱讀電子書，最後更提到維他命和食物，是個蠻與眾不同的回答。考生也可以想想其他優缺點喔，在融入自己的回答中。

PART 01 個人喜好

PART 02 二選一話題

PART 03 概述觀點

PART 04 整合文章和講座

PART 05 討論解決辦法

PART 06 概括講座內容

大學是否該提供學生娛樂

Narrator: You will now be asked to give your opinion about a familiar topic. After you read the question, you will have 15 seconds to prepare your response and 45 seconds to speak.

Task 2 "Should universities provide students with entertainment?"

▶**MP3 031**

口說 回答

請先別看後面的參考答案,自己練習一次,看自己聽到問題會如何回答這題,練習過後,可以參考書中三個回答,並將佳句記下和觀看解析,用於應考中,更無往不利。

_____

_____

_____

_____

_____

_____

_____

_____

(Prepare time: 15 seconds,Response time: 45 seconds)

PART 01 個人喜好

PART 02 二選一話題

PART 03 概述觀點

PART 04 整合文章和講座

PART 05 討論解決辦法

PART 06 概括講座內容

❶ provide funding for student entertainment

Universities should provide students with entertainment, such as movies or concerts on campus. Imagine how much stress students are under studying all day, so it's ok to just loosen up a little by watching a film right after a class…say International Law or Advanced Calculus. I just don't see the harm here. In addition, our brain needs the rest. With 8 hours of courses a day it's like the brain has reached its limit. Watching films gives the brain exactly that and **the film eases the information that students consume all day, so the brain restores itself.** Students can go home and have study a little… totally like why after you exercise, you are in the mood for studying.

大學應該要提供學生娛樂，例如在校園內有電影或音樂會。想像學生在讀了一整天的書後有多少壓力，而且在課後看電影能放鬆一下，這是ok的…像是國際法律或高階微積分課後。我不認為有什麼壞處。此外，我們的大腦需要休息。每天八小時的課程對像是大腦來說已經達到的上限了。觀看電影確切地給予大腦它所需要的，而且在**電影舒緩了學生吸收一整天的資訊後，如此一來大腦會自我復原。**學生就可以回家然後讀點書…整個像是為什麼你運動後，你會有心情讀書那樣。

❷ should not provide students with entertainment

Universities should not provide students with entertainment, such as movies or concerts on campus. It's an academic setting and can digress students a bit from studying. Students are bound to be distracted by the entertainment. Tuitions are high and they pay money to learn things so that they will equip themselves with adequate knowledge and professional techniques before they graduate. I just can't imagine a situation where professors allow students to use smartphones during the course and expect students to focus. I don't think having the entertainment will help them, and they probably think about which movie would be ideal if they are asking a girl on a date during the class…totally wrong…if they'd like to have some entertainment, **do that outside the school setting.**

大學不應該要提供學生娛樂，例如在校園內有電影或音樂會。這是學術環境，而且這會使學生學習分心。學生必定會被娛樂影響而分心。學費是高昂的而且他們是付錢去學習事情，這樣他們在畢業前才能將自己準備好，具有足夠的知識和專業技能。我就是無法想像一種情況，教授允許學生在上課期間使用智慧型手機，然後期待學生專注。我不認為有娛樂能幫助他們，而且他們可能在上課期間就在想著，如果他們要邀哪個女生去約會的話，看哪部電影會比較合適呢？…整個是錯的…如果他們想要有些娛樂的話，**在學校環境外在從事吧！**

PART 01 個人喜好

PART 02 二選一話題

PART 03 概述觀點

PART 04 整合文章和講座

PART 05 討論解決辦法

PART 06 概括講座內容

❸ provide funding for student entertainment

Universities should provide students with entertainment, such as movies or concerts on campus. Haven't you heard all work and no play makes Jack a dull boy. It's just a two-hour movie…or an hour and 40 minutes…I don't know why some professors are making a big deal about it…like if you spend that kind of time watching a film, you won't get anywhere. Keep in mind that it's just a school setting. **After you graduate who cares whether you got an A in History or an A+ in Economics.** Employers and bank just don't care. It isn't like our future rests on academic success….I will study hard, but give me the damn entertainment, too.

大學應該要提供學生娛樂，例如在校園內有電影或音樂會。你沒聽過只是工作而不遊戲會使人變得遲鈍。這只是兩小時的電影…或是一小時40分鐘…我不知道為什麼有些教授會為此小題大作…像是如果你花了那樣的時間在觀看電影上，你就不會有所成就。記住這僅是在學校環境裡頭。**在你畢業後，誰在乎你在歷史課拿到A或是在經濟學拿到A+呢？雇主和銀行就不在乎。**別弄得好像是我們的未來都要仰賴學術成功…我會認真讀書，但是也給我那該死的娛樂。

解析

　　這題是詢問大學是否該提供學生娛樂的問題。第一個回答也是很生動的回答。「這是ok的…像是國際法律或高階微積分課後。我不認為有什麼壞處。」等等都讓考官覺得這不是背稿子，像是個大學生表達對這件事的看法。後面更提到看電影舒緩了壓力等，大腦休息後更有助於學習，聽起來可圈可點。

　　第二個回答是比較老派但也並非不是道理，學生很容易分心，還有活潑地講到「而且他們可能在上課期間就在想著，如果他們要邀哪個女生去約會的話，看哪部電影會比較合適呢？…整個是錯的…」，可以讓聽太多答案的考官有時間可以笑一下或讓大腦休息一下，答案最後提到是要在校外從事比較好，整體來說答案蠻有個性，很吸引人。

　　最後一個答案蠻與眾不同的，有講到「只是工作而不遊戲會使人變得遲鈍」、「為此小題大作」、「在你畢業後，誰在乎你在歷史課拿到A或是在經濟學拿到A+呢？雇主和銀行就不在乎。別弄得好像是我們的未來都要仰賴學術成功…我會認真讀書，但是也給我那該死的娛樂。」，真的是妙答啊！（已跪）

PART 01 個人喜好
PART 02 二選一話題
PART 03 概述觀點
PART 04 整合文章和講座
PART 05 討論解決辦法
PART 06 概括講座內容

part 3

概述觀點題

概述觀點題選了校園場景中考生更容易遇到的考題，這些類型都很生活化，考生可以從自己遇到該問題，例如學校泳池關閉後，對自己會造成什麼影響等或是同學可能會怎麼評論這個事件，就可以輕易答這個類型的考題。當中僅需要注意一點，因為在傳統的學習環境中考試方式是聽完試題後寫答案，這部分的練習是聽讀說，所以掌握這個流程並大量練習後就能很快上手囉！

1 Restriction of Cycling on Campus

禁止在校內騎自行車

Narrator: you will now read a short passage on a campus situation and then listen to a talk on that same subject. Then you will be asked to answer a question from both the reading and the talk. After the question you will have 30 seconds to prepare and 60 seconds to respond.
▶MP3 033

Narrator: Best University is now debating about whether cycling on campus is too dangerous, especially after the accident. Read the article from the local newspaper, written by a news reporter. You will have 45 seconds to read the article. Begin reading now.

Reading time: 45 seconds

Simply put⋯there is no way that Best University will allow students to ride bicycles in the school⋯after an accident happened the other day⋯a student's head was severely injured⋯and is still unconscious in the hospital⋯there are still some reporters waiting outside the ICU 2⋯to see how parents are going to respond to the accident. There are simply too many meandering routes from school districts to districts⋯ it's like a bicycle racing contest and pedestrians are sometimes competing with bicycle riders for the road. Wow⋯that student has no intention of slowing down at the turn⋯which is pretty scary⋯it seems that Best University needs to take drastic measures to counter with the safety of bicycle riding in the campus⋯and the vote for "Restriction of Cycling on Campus" is this Wednesday⋯3 p.m.

(reporter, Mary Wang)

PART 01 個人喜好

PART 02 二選一話題

PART 03 概述觀點

PART 04 整合文章和講座

PART 05 討論解決辦法

PART 06 概括講座內容

Narrator: now listen to two students discussing the article. ▶MP3 034

 筆記

_____

_____

_____

_____

_____

_____

_____

口說 回答

The woman expresses her opinion about **Restriction of Cycling on Campus.** State her opinion and explain the reasons she gives for that opinion. ▶MP3 035

Prepare time: 30 seconds
Response time: 60 seconds

PART 01 個人喜好

PART 02 二選一話題

PART 03 概述觀點

PART 04 整合文章和講座

PART 05 討論解決辦法

PART 06 概括講座內容

＿＿＿＿＿＿＿＿＿＿＿＿＿＿＿＿＿＿＿＿＿＿＿＿

＿＿＿＿＿＿＿＿＿＿＿＿＿＿＿＿＿＿＿＿＿＿＿＿

＿＿＿＿＿＿＿＿＿＿＿＿＿＿＿＿＿＿＿＿＿＿＿＿

＿＿＿＿＿＿＿＿＿＿＿＿＿＿＿＿＿＿＿＿＿＿＿＿

＿＿＿＿＿＿＿＿＿＿＿＿＿＿＿＿＿＿＿＿＿＿＿＿

（準備期間內，試著在筆記欄頁上寫下幾個所想要描述的重點並搭配前面閱讀和所聽到的內容，做出接下來的回答。）

 閱讀文章 中譯

　　簡單地說…在幾天前發生的意外事件後…倍斯特大學不可能允許學生在校園內騎乘腳踏車…一位學生的頭部嚴重受創…而且在醫院仍毫無意識…仍有一些記者們在加護病房2號房外等著…看父母會如何回應這起意外事件。在學校學區跟學區域之間有著太多的彎曲道路…就像是腳踏車競賽一樣，而行人有時候與腳踏車騎乘者競爭路權。哇！…學生在轉彎時，沒有任何想要減低速度的意圖…這相當的可怕…似乎倍斯特大學需要採取急遽的措施去應對在校內騎乘腳踏車的安全性，而「禁止在校內騎自行車」的投票是這週三…下午三點鐘。

（記者，瑪莉・王）

Jim: have you seen the news yet?

Cindy: what⋯the news of the accident?

Jim: pretty horrible⋯even though I don't know him⋯ but looking at the screenshot of him lying in the hospital⋯I think we should vote against Cycling on Campus⋯

Cindy: how did that happen⋯I thought you can't film or take photos in the ICU room⋯

Jim: perhaps they pay handsomely to get that shot⋯ but that's not the main focus here⋯

Cindy: I feel bad that he got injured⋯but what about convenience? And the person who follows strict guidelines given during the announcement of the freshman campus tour⋯and the campus is just so big⋯and I'm not a marathon runner⋯I don't think I will vote against it⋯

吉姆： 你看到新聞了嗎？

辛蒂： 什麼...意外事件那則新聞嗎？

吉姆： 相當恐怖...即使我不認識他...但是看著他躺在病床上的截圖...我認為我們對於校園騎乘腳踏車一事應該要投反對票？

辛蒂： 那是怎麼發生的...我以為在加護病房裡你不能攝影或拍照...。

吉姆： 或許他們付了可觀的金額才拿到那樣子的照片...但是這不是討論的重點...。

辛蒂： 對於他受傷的部分我感到難過...但是關於腳踏車的便利性呢？而且嚴格遵守在大一新生校園導覽時的公告的騎乘者...和校園這麼大...還有我不是馬拉松跑者...我不認為我會投反對票...。

PART 01 個人喜好

PART 02 二選一話題

PART 03 概述觀點

PART 04 整合文章和講座

PART 05 討論解決辦法

PART 06 概括講座內容

參考答案 ▶MP3 036

According to the report, we are uncertain about how schools are going to respond, but it seems that the vote will be the determining factor for whether cycling will be allowed on campus or not. The woman feels bad about the accident happening, but at the same time pinpoints something like convenience, and students who follow the rules. It may be unfair for someone who follows the rules while riding a bike. Also, she mentions that the campus is too big for students. She will not vote against Cycling on Campus…

根據報導，我們對於學校會如何反應是不確定的，但是似乎投票會是校內是否允許騎乘腳踏車的決定性因素。女生對於事件的發生感到難過，但同時也指出一些像是便利性、遵守規定的學生。這可能對於某些遵守規定的騎乘者是不公平的。而且，她提到學校對於學生來說太大了。她不會對騎乘腳踏車一事投反對票。

◆ 整合能力強化

· 將短對話中文以英文口譯出來。

吉姆：　你看到新聞了嗎？

辛蒂：　什麼...意外事件那則新聞嗎？

吉姆：　相當恐怖...即使我不認識他...但是看著他躺在病床上的截圖...我認為我們對於校園騎乘腳踏車一事應該要投反對票？

辛蒂：　那是怎麼發生的...我以為在加護病房裡你不能攝影或拍照...。

吉姆：　或許他們付了可觀的金額才拿到那樣子的照片...但是這不是討論的重點...。

辛蒂：　對於他受傷的部分我感到難過...但是關於腳踏車的便利性呢？而且嚴格遵守在大一新生校園導覽時的公告的騎乘者...和校園這麼大...還有我不是馬拉松跑者...我不認為我會投反對票...。

PART 01 個人喜好

PART 02 二選一話題

PART 03 概述觀點

PART 04 整合文章和講座

PART 05 討論解決辦法

PART 06 概括講座內容

・將閱讀文章和口說參考答案以英文口譯出來。

簡單地說…在幾天前發生的意外事件後…倍斯特大學不可能允許學生在校園內騎乘腳踏車…一位學生的頭部嚴重受創…而且在醫院仍毫無意識…仍有一些記者們在加護病房2號房外等著…看父母會如何回應這起意外事件。在學校學區跟學區域之間有著太多的彎曲道路…就像是腳踏車競賽一樣，而行人有時候與腳踏車騎乘者競爭路權。哇！…學生在轉彎時，沒有任何想要減低速度的意圖…這相當的可怕…似乎倍斯特大學需要採取急遽的措施去應對在校內騎乘腳踏車的安全性，而「禁止在校內騎自行車」的投票是這週三…下午三點鐘。

（記者，瑪莉・王）

根據報導，我們對於學校會如何反應是不確定的，但是似乎投票會是校內是否允許騎乘腳踏車的決定性因素。女生對於事件的發生感到難過，但同時也指出一些像是便利性、遵守規定的學生。這可能對於某些遵守規定的騎乘者是不公平的。而且，她提到學校對於學生來說太大了。她不會對騎乘腳踏車一事投反對票。

單元字彙統整

重要字彙	
allow	允許
accident	意外
severely	嚴重地
unconscious	無意識的
hospital	醫院
ICU	加護病房
respond	回應
meandering	迂迴的
route	路線
contest	比賽
district	地區
pedestrian	行人
intention	意圖
measure	措施

PART 01 個人喜好

PART 02 二選一話題

PART 03 概述觀點

PART 04 整合文章和講座

PART 05 討論解決辦法

PART 06 概括講座內容

2 The Opening of the Coffee Shop

咖啡館開幕

Narrator: you will now read a short passage on a campus situation and then listen to a talk on that same subject. Then you will be asked to answer a question from both the reading and the talk. After the question you will have 30 seconds to prepare and 60 seconds to respond.

▶MP3 037

Narrator: Best University is planning to open a new coffee shop. Read the article from the local newspaper, written by a news reporter . You will have 45 seconds to read the article. Begin reading now.

Reading time: 45 seconds

With the new opening of the coffee shop, students are bound to have more options for many things, including foods, study venues, amazing views and so on. Students enjoy visiting this place since it's such a romantic spot, and they are expecting after taking a long walk, there should have a coffee shop so that they can take some rest or even study in there, but a few months ago somehow the boards were rejecting the idea thinking that it would not be a perfect venue for the coffee shop. Now they can almost taste the scent of lavenders if they are sitting by the window side, and they get to see the magnificent lake.

(reporter, Cindy Wang)

PART 01 個人喜好

PART 02 二選一話題

PART 03 概述觀點

PART 04 整合文章和講座

PART 05 討論解決辦法

PART 06 概括講座內容

Narrator: now listen to two students discussing the article. ▶MP3 038

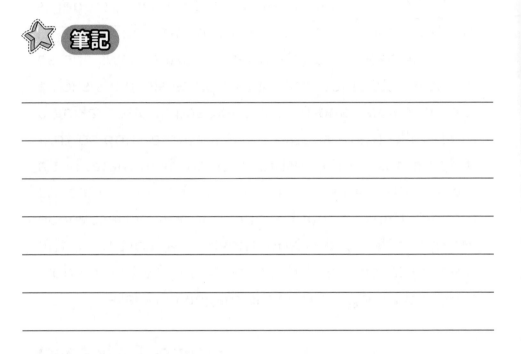

The man expresses his opinion about **the new opening of the coffee shop**. State his opinion and explain the reasons he gives for that opinion.
▶MP3 039

Prepare time: 30 seconds
Response time: 60 seconds

PART 01 個人喜好

PART 02 二選一話題

PART 03 概述觀點

PART 04 整合文章和講座

PART 05 討論解決辦法

PART 06 概括講座內容

_____

_____

_____

_____

_____

（準備期間內，試著在筆記欄頁上寫下幾個所想要描述的重點
並搭配前面閱讀和所聽到的內容，做出接下來的回答。）

閱讀文章 中譯

　　隨著咖啡店新開幕，學生對於許多事情有著更多的選擇，
包含食物、學習地點、驚人的風景等等的。既然這是如此浪漫
的景點，學生一直享受參觀這個地方，他們期待在走一長段路
後，有間咖啡店所以他們可以有地方可以休息或甚至能在那研
讀，但幾個月前基於某些原因，學校董事會拒絕這個想法，認
為這個地點不會是咖啡店的完美地點。現在他們幾乎能夠嚐到
薰衣草的香味，如果他們能夠坐在窗戶旁，而且他們能夠看到
壯觀的湖泊。

（記者，辛蒂・王）

Linda: where are you heading? The new coffee shop?

Jack: yep, since with the new opening, you get to drink the second cup of coffee for free.

Linda: wow···free···seriously?

Jack: it's so crowded there···I went to the coffee shop yesterday, and luckily they have an enlarged study room in the basement.

Linda: sounds great···perhaps I should go there some day···I heard about the romantic views.

Jack: after taking a long walk, you won't feel so dizzy after a long day at school, and the food there is relatively cheap, but more delicious than the school cafeteria.

Jack: ···and you won't have to worry about safety if you are taking the long trail with me···so what do you think?

琳達： 你要去哪裡？新的咖啡店嗎？

傑克： 是的，因為隨著咖啡店新開幕，喝第二杯咖啡免費。

琳達： 哇!...免費...真的嗎？

傑克： 這裡好擁擠喔...我昨天去咖啡店，而幸運地是他們地下室有加大的讀書室。

琳達： 聽起來很棒...或許我有天應該要去那裡...我聽說了那裡的浪漫景點。

傑克： 在走一長段路後，你不會因為在學校一整天後感到暈眩，而且那裡的食物相對來說便宜，但是比起學校餐館更美味。

傑克： ...你不用擔心安全的部分，如果你是跟我一起走那長長的小徑...所以妳覺得呢？

The reporter informs all students about the opening of the new coffee shop and tells them that there are several benefits, such as a study venue, food, and amazing views. The man in the conversation is welcoming the changes. He mentions several advantages regarding the new opening, such as the second cup of coffee is free. In addition, the new coffee shop has an enlarged study room in the basement so that students will have enough room to study. Also, taking a long trail improves a person's overall mood and health. You won't feel dizziness after sitting in the classroom all day, and it can boost your ability to learn.

記者告知所有學生關於咖啡店新開幕的事情，而且告訴他們會有幾個好處，例如學習的場所、食物和驚人的景色。對話中的男子很歡迎這樣子的改變。她提到關於新開幕的幾個優點，例如享用第二杯咖啡是免費的。此外，新開幕的咖啡店在地下室有加大的讀書室，所以學生會有足夠的空間研讀。而且，步行長小徑改進一個人整體的心情和健康。你不會因為在教室待整天而感到暈眩，而且這能提升妳學習能力。

整合能力強化

・將短對話中文以英文口譯出來。

琳達：　你要去哪裡？新的咖啡店嗎？

傑克：　是的，因為隨著咖啡店新開幕，喝第二杯咖啡免費。

琳達：　哇!...免費...真的嗎？

傑克：　這裡好擁擠喔...我昨天去咖啡店，而幸運地是他們地下室有加大的讀書室。

琳達：　聽起來很棒...或許我有天應該要去那裡...我聽說了那裡的浪漫景點。

傑克：　在走一長段路後，你部會因為在學校一整天後感到暈眩，而且那裡的食物相對來説便宜，但是比起學校餐館更美味。

傑克：　...你不用擔心安全的部分，如果你是跟我一起走那長長的小徑...所以妳覺得呢？

PART 01 個人喜好

PART 02 二選一話題

PART 03 概述觀點

PART 04 整合文章和講座

PART 05 討論解決辦法

PART 06 概括講座內容

· 將閱讀文章和口說參考答案以英文口譯出來。

　　隨著咖啡店新開幕，學生對於許多事情有著更多的選擇，包含食物、學習地點、驚人的風景等等的。既然這是如此浪漫的景點，學生一直享受參觀這個地方，他們期待在走一長段路後，有間咖啡店所以他們可以有地方可以休息或甚至能在那研讀，但幾個月前基於某些原因，學校董事會拒絕這個想法，認為這個地點不會是咖啡店的完美地點。現在他們幾乎能夠嚐到薰衣草的香味，如果他們能夠坐在窗戶旁，而且他們能夠看到壯觀的湖泊。

（記者，辛蒂·王）

　　記者告知所有學生關於咖啡店新開幕的事情，而且告訴他們會有幾個好處，例如學習的場所、食物和驚人的景色。對話中的男子很歡迎這樣子的改變。她提到關於新開幕的幾個優點，例如享用第二杯咖啡是免費的。此外，新開幕的咖啡店在地下室有加大的讀書室，所以學生會有足夠的空間研讀。而且，步行長小徑改進一個人整體的心情和健康。你不會因為在教室待整天而感到暈眩，而且這能提升妳學習能力。

單元字彙 統整

重要字彙	
new	新的
opening	開幕
coffee	咖啡
shop	店
are bound to	一定
option	選擇
venue	場所
view	景色
romantic	浪漫的
spot	地點
expect	期待
reject	拒絕
perfect	完美的
lavender	薰衣草

PART 01　個人喜好

PART 02　二選一話題

PART 03　概述觀點

PART 04　整合文章和講座

PART 05　討論解決辦法

PART 06　概括講座內容

3 Cancellation of Magazine Publication

學校雜誌取消發行

Narrator: you will now read a short passage on a campus situation and then listen to a talk on that same subject. Then you will be asked to answer a question from both the reading and the talk. After the question you will have 30 seconds to prepare and 60 seconds to respond.
▶ MP3 041

Narrator: Best University is thinking about cancelling magazine publication. Read the article from the school's website, written by the school principal. You will have 45 seconds to read the article. Begin reading now.

Reading time: 45 seconds

This was an announcement made by the school principal. Best University has been proud of differentiating itself from other universities by having several practical facilities, such as printing plants and magazine buildings. Students will learn the most practical things from working there…during four years of studying… However, due to a tight budget and a shortage of students these years, Best Fashion No.566 will be the last issue, which means there won't be having a weekly magazine for Best University students to read. According to several students, cancellation of the magazine publication will harm the recruitment for next year's students, since people enrolling Best University are eyeing for the job opportunity of working in the printing plants and magazine buildings.

PART 01 個人喜好
PART 02 二選一話題
PART 03 概述觀點
PART 04 整合文章和講座
PART 05 討論解決辦法
PART 06 概括講座內容

Narrator: now listen to two students discussing the article. ▶MP3 042

 筆記

_____

_____

_____

_____

_____

_____

口說 回答

The woman expresses her opinion about **cancellation of the magazine publication.** State her opinion and explain the reasons she gives for that opinion.
▶MP3 043

Prepare time: 30 seconds
Response time: 60 seconds

PART 01 個人喜好

PART 02 二選一話題

PART 03 概述觀點

PART 04 整合文章和講座

PART 05 討論解決辦法

PART 06 概括講座內容

_____

_____

_____

_____

_____

_____

（準備期間內，試著在筆記欄頁上寫下幾個所想要描述的重點並搭配前面閱讀和所聽到的內容，做出接下來的回答。）

 閱讀文章 中譯

　　這是由學校校長所發佈的公告。倍斯特大學一直對於有著幾個實用的設施，例如印刷廠和雜誌大樓，而能夠與其他大學區隔化這點感到引以為傲。四年的學習期間…學生會學習到最實用的東西…。然而，近幾年，由於緊縮的預算和學生短缺，倍斯特時尚雜誌第566期將會是最後一期，這意謂著不再有每兩周發行的雜誌提供給倍斯特大學學生閱讀。根據幾個學生，取消雜誌的出版會損害明年學生的招募，因為學生會註冊倍斯特大學目光是著眼於能在印刷廠和雜誌大樓的工作機會。

Mary: I can't believe they are cancelling the publication of the magazine. I've been working my ass off to get the summer internship…

Jack: sounds fine with me…not interested in fashion and related stuff…

Mary: to you maybe… because you are a guy…but they are destroying every girl's dream…and imagine how many girls are in this school…

Jack: just grab some drinks and tomorrow it's the same day

Mary: I hope they will think twice…perhaps by changing this from a weekly publication to biweekly…or someone can finance the school so that they won't cancel…

Jack: nowadays people read those things through social networking sites…just forget it…let me buy you another drink…I heard there is a new opening…

瑪莉：　我不敢相信他們取消了雜誌的出版。我已經盡我所能地拿到暑期工讀的機會了。

傑克：　對我來説聽起來還好…對於時尚和相關的東西不感興趣。

瑪莉：　對你來説或許是這樣…因為你是男人…但是他們會破壞每個女孩的夢想…想像這間學校有多少女孩…。

傑克：　就喝幾杯吧…明天又是相同的日子。

瑪莉：　我希望他們應該要三思…或許藉將每週出版雜誌改成每雙週出版…或是有些人可以以財政資助學校，這樣學校就不會取消了…。

傑克：　現在每個人透過社交網路平台讀那些東西…所以忘了吧…讓我請你喝另一杯酒…我聽説有個新開幕的…。

PART 01 個人喜好

PART 02 二選一話題

PART 03 概述觀點

PART 04 整合文章和講座

PART 05 討論解決辦法

PART 06 概括講座內容

The school announces that Best Fashion No.566 will be the last issue, even though it's what the school has been known for. Like several students, the woman in the conversation feels bad about the situation. She expects to learn new things from working there, and she has been working hard to get the summer internship. She is hoping that things will turn around…perhaps not be so drastic… the school can adjust the publication by turning it into a biweekly magazine or someone can finance the school so that the magazine will not be cancelled.

學校宣布倍斯特時尚雜誌第566期將會是最後一期，即使這是學校引以聞名的部分。像是幾個學生一樣，聽力中的女生對於這個情況感到難過。她期待能從那裡的工作經驗中學習事情，而且她一直很努力才獲選暑期工讀的機會。她希望事情能有轉圜餘地…或許不要那麼急遽…學校能調整出版時程，將雜誌轉成兩週出版或是某個人可以資助學校，這樣子雜誌就不會遭到取消。

 整合能力強化

· 將短對話中文以英文口譯出來。

瑪莉： 我不敢相信他們取消了雜誌的出版。我已經盡我所能地
　　　 拿到暑期工讀的機會了。

傑克： 對我來說聽起來還好…對於時尚和相關的東西不感興
　　　 趣。

瑪莉： 對你來說或許是這樣…因為你是男人…但是他們會破壞
　　　 每個女孩的夢想…想像這間學校有多少女孩…。

傑克： 就喝幾杯吧…明天有是相同的日子。

瑪莉： 我希望他們應該要三思…或許藉將每週出版雜誌改成每
　　　 雙週出版…或是有些人可以以財政資助學校，這樣學校
　　　 就不會取消了…。

傑克： 現在每個人透過社交網路平台讀那些東西…所以忘了
　　　 吧…讓我請你喝另一杯酒…我聽說有個新開幕的…。

PART 01 個人喜好

PART 02 二選一話題

PART 03 概述觀點

PART 04 整合文章和講座

PART 05 討論解決辦法

PART 06 概括講座內容

・將閱讀文章和口說參考答案以英文口譯出來。

　　這是由學校校長所發佈的公告。倍斯特大學一直對於有著幾個實用的設施，例如印刷廠和雜誌大樓，而能夠與其他大學區隔化這點感到引以為傲。四年的學習期間…學生會學習到最實用的東西…。然而，近幾年，由於緊縮的預算和學生短缺，倍斯特時尚雜誌第566期將會是最後一期，這意謂著不再有每兩周發行的雜誌提供給倍斯特大學學生閱讀。根據幾個學生，取消雜誌的出版會損害明年學生的招募，因為學生會註冊倍斯特大學目光是著眼於能在印刷廠和雜誌大樓的工作機會。

　　學校宣布倍斯特時尚雜誌第566期將會是最後一期，即使這是學校引以聞名的部分。像是幾個學生一樣，聽力中的女生對於這個情況感到難過。她期待能從那裡的工作經驗中學習事情，而且她一直很努力才獲選暑期工讀的機會。她希望事情能有轉圜餘地…或許不要那麼急遽…學校能調整出版時程，將雜誌轉成兩週出版或是某個人可以資助學校，這樣子雜誌就不會遭到取消。

單元字彙統整

重要字彙	
announcement	公告
principal	校長
differentiate	區隔化
several	幾個
practical	實用的
facility	設施
plant	廠
magazine	雜誌
budget	預算
shortage	短缺
issue	期
cancellation	取消
publication	出版
recruitment	招募

PART 01 個人喜好

PART 02 二選一話題

PART 03 概述觀點

PART 04 整合文章和講座

PART 05 討論解決辦法

PART 06 概括講座內容

UNIT 4

Extension of Marine Biology Museum

海洋生物博物館延長開館時間

Narrator: you will now read a short passage on a campus situation and then listen to a talk on that same subject. Then you will be asked to answer a question from both the reading and the talk. After the question you will have 30 seconds to prepare and 60 seconds to respond.
▶ **MP3 045**

Narrator: Best University has some considerations when it comes to extension of marine biology museum. Read the article from the local newspaper, written by a news reporter. You will have 45 seconds to read the article. Begin reading now.

Reading time: 45 seconds

Students majoring in marine biology gathered at the entrance of Marine Biology Museum demanding the extension of the opening hour, according to our earlier report. However, Best University maintains that it will add additional costs for the overall operation and there are other concerns, too. The safety concern for marine creatures and students has been one of the reasons that the board of Best University votes against the extension. Students can fully use the opening hours to do the research they need, according to one of the professors at Best University. There is simply no need for the extension⋯the final announcement at the school bulletin board concords the previous announcement that there won't be any extension for the museum.

(Reporter: Mark Chen)

01 個人喜好
02 二選一話題
03 概述觀點
04 整合文章和講座
05 討論解決辦法
06 概括講座內容

Narrator: now listen to two students discussing the article. ▶MP3 046

_____

_____

_____

_____

_____

_____

The man expresses his opinion about extension of Marine Biology Museum Hours. State his opinion and explain the reasons his gives for that opinion.
▶MP3 047

Prepare time: 30 seconds
Response time: 60 seconds

PART 01 個人喜好

PART 02 二選一話題

PART 03 概述觀點

PART 04 整合文章和講座

PART 05 討論解決辦法

PART 06 概括講座內容

_____

_____

_____

_____

_____

（準備期間內，試著在筆記欄頁上寫下幾個所想要描述的重點並搭配前面閱讀和所聽到的內容，做出接下來的回答。）

閱讀文章 中譯

　　主修生物學的學生聚集在海洋生物博物館的入口處要求延長開館的時間，根據我們稍早前的報導。然而，倍斯特大學宣稱此舉將會增加整體營運的額外的花費，而且還有其他考量在內。海洋生物和學生們的安全性考量一直是倍斯特大學董事會對此一直投反對票的原因之一。學生能夠充分利用開館的時間去做他們所需要的研究，根據倍斯特大學其中一位教授。沒有延長博物館營運時間的需要…最後在學校公布欄公佈的資訊與先前的公告一致，也就是不會延長博物館營運的時間。

(馬克‧陳)

Linda: I can't believe there won't be any extension. It's too cruel…I just can't get up that early…normally I go there around lunch time…

Jack: perhaps you should wake up early…and I don't think the museum should be extended…14 hours a day is long enough…plus school assignments are not that exhausted…you know

Linda: perhaps…some marine creatures are easily disturbed…

Jack: Yep…it will cause more problems for the staff, if it opens longer than the existing hours. I worked in the museum last summer…lots of things going on in there…and if you haven't had that kind of working experiences…you will assume that it's kind of OK…therefore, I am thinking that the school is doing the right thing.

PART 01 個人喜好

PART 02 二選一話題

PART 03 概述觀點

PART 04 整合文章和講座

PART 05 討論解決辦法

PART 06 概括講座內容

琳達： 我不敢相信博物館不會延長時間。這太殘忍了…我沒辦法這麼早起…通常我午餐時段左右才會到博物館。

傑克： 或許你該早點起來…而且我不認為博物館該延長…每天14小時已經夠長了…再說學校的課業沒有那麼累…你知道的。

琳達： 或許…有些海洋生物會很容易受到擾動。

傑克： 是的…這對於員工來說也會引起更多問題，如果開館的時間長於現有的時間的話。我去年夏天在博物館工作…那裡發生了許多事情…而且如果你沒有那樣子的工作經驗的話…你會假定延長時段是可行的…因此我認為學校是做了對了決定。

From the final announcement at the school bulletin board, there won't be any extension for the museum. The man in the conversation expresses a different opinion from the woman, thinking that the museum should not be extended. It's already opened for 14 hours a day, and school assignments don't require you to be in that place for long periods of time. In addition, there are other concerns. Some marine creatures are easily disturbed. If its opening hours are longer, the problem for the staff will be greater. Also, from his working experiences last summer, he knows what it's going to be like in there, so he thinks that the school makes the right decision for not extending the time.

從學校公佈欄的最後公告中可以得知，博物館不會延長時段。聽力中的男子表達了不同的於女子的看法，認為博物館應該不要延長時段。博物館每日經營時段已經14小時了，而且學校作業不需要長時間待在博物館內。此外，還有其他考量在。有些海洋生物很容易受到擾動。如果開幕的時段較長，對於員工所要負擔的問題就更重大。而且，從他去年的工作經驗來看，他知道那裡會有什麼情況發生，所以他認為學校對於不延長博物館營業時段是做了正確的決定。

PART 01 個人喜好

PART 02 二選一話題

PART 03 概述觀點

PART 04 整合文章和講座

PART 05 討論解決辦法

PART 06 概括講座內容

整合能力強化

·將短對話中文以英文口譯出來。

琳達： 我不敢相信博物館不會延長時間。這太殘忍了…我沒辦法這麼早起…通常我午餐時段左右才會到博物館。

傑克： 或許你該早點起來…而且我不認為博物館該延長…每天14小時已經夠長了…再說學校的課業沒有那麼累…你知道的。

琳達： 或許…有些海洋生物會很容易受到擾動。

傑克： 是的…這對於員工來說也會引起更多問題，如果開館的時間長於現有的時間的話。我去年夏天在博物館工作…那裡發生了許多事情…而且如果你沒有那樣子的工作經驗的話…你會假定延長時段是可行的…因此我認為學校是做了對了決定。

‧將閱讀文章和口說參考答案以英文口譯出來。

　　主修生物學的學生聚集在海洋生物學博物館的入口處要求延長開館的時間，根據我們稍早前的報導。然而，倍斯特大學宣稱此舉將會增加整體營運的額外的花費，而且還有其他考量在內。海洋生物和學生們的安全性考量一直是倍斯特大學董事會對此一直投反對票的原因之一。學生能夠充分利用開館的時間去做他們所需要的研究，根據倍斯特大學其中一位教授。沒有延長博物館營運時間的需要…最後在學校公布欄公佈的資訊與先前的公告一致，也就是不會延長博物館營運的時間。

　　從學校公佈欄的最後公告中可以得知，博物館不會延長時段。聽力中的男子表達了不同的於女子的看法，認為博物館應該不要延長時段。博物館每日經營時段已經14小時了，而且學校作業不需要長時間待在博物館內。此外，還有其他考量在。有些海洋生物很容易受到擾動。如果開幕的時段較長，對於員工所要負擔的問題就更重大。而且，從他去年的工作經驗來看，他知道那裡會有什麼情況發生，所以他認為學校對於不延長博物館營業時段是做了正確的決定。

單元字彙統整

重要字彙	
major	主修
biology	生物學
gather	聚集
entrance	入口
marine	海洋的
museum	博物館
demand	要求
extension	延長
overall	整體的
concern	關注
board	董事會
opening	開幕
research	研究
concord	一致

PART 01 個人喜好

PART 02 二選一話題

PART 03 概述觀點

PART 04 整合文章和講座

PART 05 討論解決辦法

PART 06 概括講座內容

5

The Closing of the Swimming Pool

游泳池關閉

Narrator: you will now read a short passage on a campus situation and then listen to a talk on that same subject. Then you will be asked to answer a question from both the reading and the talk. After the question you will have 30 seconds to prepare and 60 seconds to respond.
▶ **MP3 049**

Narrator: Best University made an announcement that the swimming pool will be closed in a few days. Read the article from the local newspaper, written by a news reporter. You will have 45 seconds to read the article. Begin reading now.

Reading time: 45 seconds

The swimming pool will be closed in just a few days, says students at Best University. There are lots of reasons behind the closing. It's more than just being too old. Sexual harassment lawsuit has cost Best University millions of dollars⋯ Other than the sexual harassment, chlorine concentrations are above the normal standard, which seems to be the main reason that the swimming pool should be closed. It wasn't until that lifeguards called an ambulance that the school admitted to the press that several students were having breathing difficulties during swimming. The domestic news calls this the worst time for Best University⋯, and it's sweltering hot outside, I'm sure students are not happy about the closure of the swimming pool.

(Reporter: Judy Lin)

PART 01 個人喜好

PART 02 二選一話題

PART 03 概述觀點

PART 04 整合文章和講座

PART 05 討論解決辦法

PART 06 概括講座內容

Narrator: now listen to two students discussing the article. ▶MP3 050

 筆記

_____

_____

_____

_____

_____

_____

口說 回答

The woman expresses her opinion about the closing of the swimming pool. State her opinion and explain the reasons she gives for that opinion. ▶MP3 051

Prepare time: 30 seconds
Response time: 60 seconds

PART 01 個人喜好

PART 02 二選一話題

03 概述觀點

PART 04 整合文章和講座

PART 05 討論解決辦法

PART 06 概括講座內容

_____

_____

_____

_____

_____

（準備期間內，試著在筆記欄頁上寫下幾個所想要描述的重點
並搭配前面閱讀和所聽到的內容，做出接下來的回答。）

閱讀文章 中譯

　　游泳池將於幾天內關閉，一名倍斯特大學學生說道。對於
泳池關閉背後有許多原因。不僅僅是太老舊。性騷擾纏訟官司
已經使得倍斯特大學耗資幾百萬美元的金錢…。而除了性騷擾
外，泳池中氯濃度含量高於一般標準，這似乎是泳池應該關閉
的主要原因。直到救生員們叫救護車後，學校才向新聞媒體承
認有幾個學生在游泳期間有呼吸困難的症狀出現。國內新聞稱
這則新聞為倍斯特大學最糟的時刻…，而且現在外頭正酷熱難
耐，我相信學生對於泳池關閉的事件一定不太開心。

（記者，茱蒂‧林）

Jack: it's front page news···how can so many bad things all happen at once···I mean one of these days··· but thank god···I don't swim···

Cindy: I can't believe the swimming pool will no longer be used···what about the membership and the courses···and it's so hot out there···you know how swimming helps students relax···

Jack: perhaps it's the best for the students···imagine the amount of chlorine you overconsume···

Cindy: no wonder I sometimes feel a little dizzy and like vomiting or something···but I'm not pregnant···I guess some of the classmates mistakenly think I'm pregnant···now it is all clear···the culprit is chlorine. I think we deserve a swimming pool with the right amount of chlorine.

傑克： 這是頭條新聞了…怎麼許多糟糕的事情都同時發生了…我指的是這幾天…但是謝天謝地…我不會游泳。

辛蒂： 我不敢相信游泳池不能再使用了…那關於會員和學校課程呢…外頭這麼炎熱…你知道游泳能幫助學生放鬆…

傑克： 或許這對於學生來說是最棒的了…想像妳過度攝取了多少氯的量…。

辛蒂： 難怪我有時候會覺得有點暈眩而且像是有想吐的感覺或什麼的…但並不是因為我懷孕了…我想有些同學誤以為我懷孕了…現在事情真相大白了…罪魁禍首是氯氣。我認為我們值得一個加入適量氯的游泳池。

PART 01 個人喜好

PART 02 二選一話題

PART 03 概述觀點

PART 04 整合文章和講座

PART 05 討論解決辦法

PART 06 概括講座內容

Students are aware that the swimming pool will be closed in just a few days. The woman in the conversation thinks there are several advantages of going to the swimming pool. It cools people down since the weather is hot outside the classroom. In addition, swimming helps people relax. The downside of the swimming is consuming too much chlorine, and she is having symptoms like vomiting. The hilarious part is that she is mistakenly thought of as a pregnant woman. Finally, she thinks students deserve to be treated better.

學生查覺到游泳池會於幾天內就關閉了。女子在會話中認為游泳池會有幾項優點。它能使學生們感到冷靜,既然教室外頭那麼炎熱。此外,游泳幫助人們放鬆。游泳池的缺點是會攝入過多的氯氣,而她有了嘔吐的症狀。最好笑的部分是她被誤當成懷孕的女人。最後她認為學生值得更好的對待。

整合能力強化

·將短對話中文以英文口譯出來。

傑克： 這是頭條新聞了…怎麼許多糟糕的事情都同時發生了…我指的是這幾天…但是謝天謝地…我不會游泳。

辛蒂： 我不敢相信游泳池不再使用了…那關於會員和學校課程呢…外頭這麼炎熱…你知道游泳能幫助學生放鬆…

傑克： 或許這對於學生來説是最棒的了…想像妳過度攝取了多少氯的量…。

辛蒂： 難怪我有時候會覺得有點暈眩而且有想吐的感覺或什麼的…但並不是因為我懷孕了…我想有些同學誤以為我懷孕了…現在事情真相大白了…罪魁禍首是氯氣。我認為我們值得一個加入適量氯的游泳池。

PART 01 個人喜好

PART 02 二選一話題

PART 03 概述觀點

PART 04 整合文章和講座

PART 05 討論解決辦法

PART 06 概括講座內容

・將閱讀文章和口說參考答案以英文口譯出來。

　　游泳池將於幾天內關閉，一名倍斯特大學學生説道。對於泳池關閉背後有許多原因。不僅僅是太老舊。性騷擾纏訟官司已經使得倍斯特大學耗資幾百萬美元的金錢…。而除了性騷擾外，泳池中氯濃度含量高於一班標準，這似乎是泳池應該關閉的主要原因。直到救生員們叫救護車後，學校才向新聞媒體承認有幾個學生在游泳期間有呼吸困難的症狀出現。國內新聞稱這則新聞為倍斯特大學最糟的時刻…，而且現在外頭正酷熱難耐，我相信學生對於泳池關閉的事件一定不太開心。

（記者，茉蒂・林）

　　學生查覺到游泳池會於幾天內就關閉了。女子在會話中認為游泳池會有幾項優點。它能使學生們感到冷靜，既然教室外頭那麼炎熱。此外，游泳幫助人們放鬆。游泳池的缺點是會攝入過多的氯氣，而她有了嘔吐的症狀。最好笑的部分是她被誤當成懷孕的女人。最後她認為學生值得更好的對待。

單元字彙統整

重要字彙	
pool	游泳池
reason	理由
closing	關閉
sexual	性方面的
harassment	騷擾
lawsuit	訴訟
chlorine	氯
concentration	濃度
normal	正常的
standard	標準
lifeguard	救生員
ambulance	救護車
admit	坦承
sweltering	悶熱的

PART 01 個人喜好

PART 02 二選一話題

PART 03 概述觀點

PART 04 整合文章和講座

PART 05 討論解決辦法

PART 06 概括講座內容

part 4
整合文章
及講座題

整合文章和講座題的流程和概述觀
點題相同，都是聽讀説，但是因為
討論的是學術場景的主題，有些主
題其實考生較不熟悉，會進而影響
臨場反應能力。在聽這個part的時
候要特別留神，將關鍵的重點記下
並且集中精神讀試題，再將論點以
口説的方式表達出來即可。

Procrastination

從「創新者」一書討論延遲

Narrator: you will now read a short passage and then listen to a talk on the same academic topic. You will then be asked a question about them. After you hear the question, you will have 30 seconds to prepare your response and 60 seconds to speak.

Narrator: now read the passage about **procrastination.** You will have 45 seconds to read the passage. Begin reading now. ▶ **MP3 053**

Unit 1　Procrastination
從「創新者」一書討論延遲

PART 01 個人喜好

PART 02 二選一話題

PART 03 概述觀點

PART 04 整合文章和講座

PART 05 討論解決辦法

PART 06 概括講座內容

Reading time: 45 seconds

Procrastination

In our life, we have been urged not to procrastinate. It's like procrastination is a sin that all of us all need to avoid so that we can have a better life. But in "Originals", the author offers some insights that it is not what you think. Although we are advised to do things ahead of schedules, the benefits of procrastination are usually ignored. Procrastination is not usually a bad thing. "procrastination might be conducive to originality".

Narrator: now listen to part of a lecture on this topic in the psychology class. ▶MP3 054

 筆記

_____

_____

_____

_____

_____

_____

口說 回答

Explain how the example from the professor's lecture gives us another idea about Procrastination.
▶MP3 055

Preparation Time: 30 seconds
Response Time: 60 seconds

PART 01 個人喜好

PART 02 二選一話題

PART 03 概述觀點

PART 04 整合文章和講座

PART 05 討論解決辦法

PART 06 概括講座內容

_____

_____

_____

_____

_____

_____

（準備期間內，試著在筆記欄頁上寫下幾個所想要描述的重點並搭配前面閱讀和所聽到的內容，做出接下來的回答。）

 閱讀文章 中譯

延遲

仕我們生命中，我們一直被規勸「別讓事情延遲」。這像是說著延遲對我們所有人來說是罪惡，而我們都需要避免這件事的發生，我們才能有著更美好的生活。但是在「創新者」一書，作者提供了一些洞察，表示這不是你所想的那樣。儘管我們受到建議是把事情都安排在時程前，延遲的好處卻通常是我們所忽略的。延遲通常不是件壞事。「延遲可能會有助於創新」。

In the book, we are learning that procrastination can be a good thing, especially if it's about creating something or doing something creative. Like what we have frequently heard⋯you cannot rush art. It certainly takes quite some time to produce an amazing piece. In the book, it reveals that "procrastination may be the enemy of productivity, but it can be a resource of creativity." It's true if you procrastinate, productivity will inevitably decline to a certain degree. Most of the time, your employer expects you to focus on productivity, but productivity leaves you no room to procrastinate. And you won't get the chance to think about an amazing product to be produced. The author mentions Mona Lisa as an example to show that Leonardo procrastinated for this incredible thing to be produced. He was focusing his time on doing things irrelevant to the work. But for some reason, those things are quite vital to his creation of the Mona Lisa. So from this example, you can get another idea about procrastination. Fixating on getting things done will finish a piece of work, but it will quite unlikely produce something great.

PART 01 個人喜好

PART 02 二選一話題

PART 03 概述觀點

PART 04 整合文章和講座

PART 05 討論解決辦法

PART 06 概括講座內容

在這本書中，我們學習到延遲可能會是件好事，尤其這是關於創造一些事情或做一些更具有創意性的事。像是我們通常都聽到…你不能趕藝術。這確實會花費相當的時間去產出一個驚人的作品。在書中，這接露著「延遲可能會是產量的敵人，但卻是創意的來源。」大多數時候，你的雇主期待你將重心放在產量上，但是產量讓你沒有任何可以延遲的空間。你沒有機會去思考一件驚人產品是如何產出的。作者提到蒙娜麗莎為例子，展示出李奧納多延遲讓驚人的作品能夠產出。他將時間放在製作與作品無關的事情上。但是基於一些原因，那些東西對於他呈現出蒙娜麗莎的作品創作是相當重要的。所以從這個例子中，你對於延遲有著另一個看法了。太執著於要完成某件作品，卻可能很難產出偉大的作品。

In describing procrastination, the professor uses some ideas from the book originals. Contrary to our current thinking that procrastination will make our schedules delayed, the function of procrastination can be quite surprising, especially when it comes to producing something creative. It certainly takes quite some time to produce an amazing piece of work. Procrastination sounds like a digression for you to mediate. During the process, you can come up with something great, but that kind of things will not be produced, if you are so fixated on getting it done in a specific time frame. It certainly offers us some insights to think about.

在描述延遲，教授使用了創新者一書的一些想法。與我們現有思考不同的是，延遲會使我們的進度延後，延遲的功能卻是相當驚人，尤其是當提到創作一些驚人的作品時。這確實需要花費相當的時間才能產出一件驚人的作品。延遲聽起來像是離題所以你有時間去沉思。在這過程中，你能夠想出一些出眾的想法，但是那樣子的東西不會產出，如果你過於執著要在特定的時間內要完成某件事的話。這確實提供了我們一些洞察力去思考。

◇ 整合能力強化

・使用口說題「閱讀」原文強化「寫作」能力。

　　在我們生命中，我們一直被規勸「別讓事情延遲」。這像是說著延遲對我們所有人來說是罪惡，而我們都需要避免這件事的發生，我們才能有著更美好的生活。但是在「創新者」一書，作者提供了一些洞察，表示這不是你所想的那樣。儘管我們受到建議是把事情都安排在時程前，延遲的好處卻通常是我們所忽略的。延遲通常不是件壞事。「延遲可能會有助於創新」。

PART 01 個人喜好

PART 02 二選一話題

PART 03 概述觀點

PART 04 整合文章和講座

PART 05 討論解決辦法

PART 06 概括講座內容

・使用口說題聽力原文練習影子跟讀，「口說」強化「聽力」能力。

In the book, we are learning that procrastination can be a good thing, especially if it's about creating something or doing something creative. Like what we have frequently heard⋯you cannot rush art. It certainly takes quite some time to produce an amazing piece. In the book, it reveals that "procrastination may be the enemy of productivity, but it can be a resource of creativity." It's true if you procrastinate, productivity will inevitably decline to a certain degree. Most of the time, your employer expects you to focus on productivity, but productivity leaves you no room to procrastinate. And you won't get the chance to think about an amazing product to be produced. The author mentions the Mona Lisa as an example to show that Leonardo procrastinated for this incredible thing to be produced. He was focusing his time on doing things irrelevant to the work. But for some reason, those things are quite vital to his creation of the Mona Lisa. So from this example, you can get another idea about procrastination. Fixating on getting things done will finish a piece of work, but it will quite unlikely produce something great.

・使用口說題參考答案強化「口譯」和「口說」能力。

在描述延遲，教授使用了創新者一書的一些想法。與我們現有思考不同的是，延遲會使我們的進度延後，延遲的功能卻是相當驚人，尤其是當提到創作一些驚人的作品時。這確實需要花費相當的時間才能產出一件驚人的作品。延遲聽起來像是離題所以你有時間去沉思。在這過程中，你能夠想出一些出眾的想法，但是那樣子的東西不會產出，如果你過於執著要在特定的時間內要完成某件事的話。這確實提供了我們一些洞察力去思考。

PART 01 個人喜好

PART 02 二選一話題

PART 03 概述觀點

PART 04 整合文章和講座

PART 05 討論解決辦法

PART 06 概括講座內容

2 The influence of toxins
毒素的影響

Narrator: you will now read a short passage and then listen to a talk on the same academic topic. You will then be asked a question about them. After you hear the question, you will have 30 seconds to prepare your response and 60 seconds to speak.

Narrator: now read the passage about **toxins.** You will have 45 seconds to read the passage. Begin reading now.
▶ MP3 057

Reading time: 45 seconds

Toxins

We are amazed by how toxins can kill a life in an instant. Animals and plants do produce toxins to protect themselves. Insects will avoid plants whose leaves or stems contain harmful chemicals, and plants can prevent themselves from being eaten so that they can ensure their survival and so on. Animals, like plants, have a similar mechanism. Some possess poisonous toxins so that they can paralyze and take down preys. Although toxins not always work, it can be seen as a powerful tool in the natural world.

PART 01 個人喜好

PART 02 二選一話題

PART 03 概述觀點

PART 04 整合文章和講座

PART 05 討論解決辦法

PART 06 概括講座內容

Narrator: now listen to part of a lecture on this topic in a physiology class. ▶MP3 058

筆記

_____

_____

_____

_____

_____

_____

_____

 口說 回答

Explain how the example from the professor's lecture shows the toxins can influence a body. ▶MP3 059

Preparation Time: 30 seconds
Response Time: 60 seconds

PART 01 個人喜好

PART 02 二選一話題

PART 03 概述觀點

PART 04 整合文章和講座

PART 05 討論解決辦法

PART 06 概括講座內容

_____

_____

_____

_____

_____

（準備期間內，試著在筆記欄頁上寫下幾個所想要描述的重點並搭配前面閱讀和所聽到的內容，做出接下來的回答。）

 閱讀文章 中譯

毒素

　　我們對於毒素如何能即刻殺死一個生命感到驚人。動物和植物都能產生毒素來保護自己。昆蟲會避開葉子或莖含有有害化學物質的植物，而且植物能夠避免自己本身免於被食用，所以他們可以確保自己本身的生存等等。動物，像是植物一樣有著相似的機制。有的擁有有毒的毒素所以他們能夠癱瘓或打倒獵物。儘管毒素並不是總是能發揮作用，在自然界，它可以被視為是有力的工具。

We all know what toxins produced by spiders and other creatures can do to our body. Toxins damage our body tissues. Some harm our body tissues, so our body cannot function properly. Some cause organ dysfunction, such as renal failure. We cannot metabolize those toxins. That's why we need an injection of certain antibiotics or chemicals so that our body's immune system can resume working. Some toxins are too powerful, and sometimes we cannot get the treatment in time to save ourselves. Sometimes milk or a large amount of water can dilute the concentration of the toxins in our blood vessels. Our blood vessels are very important to us since they carry oxygen, carbon dioxide, and many important gases. If the blood vessels are blocked or contain toxins, they are not able to function properly. So for your own health, do not eat unknown plants, especially plants with bright, colorful colors. And beware of any harmful insects, if you are out in the woods, otherwise, you might find yourself in the emergency room waiting for the doctor to remove those toxins from your blood vessels.

PART 01　個人喜好

PART 02　二選一話題

PART 03　概述觀點

PART 04　整合文章和講座

PART 05　討論解決辦法

PART 06　概括講座內容

　　我們都知道由蜘蛛和其他生物所產生的毒素能對我們身體產生什麼作用。毒素損害我們的身體組織。有些毒素傷害我們身體組織所以我們身體無法正常運作。有些毒素會導致組織功能不全，例如腎臟衰竭。我們無法代謝那些毒素。這就是為什麼我們需要注射特定的抗體或化學物質，所以我們身體的免疫系統能夠回復到正常的運作。有些毒素太強大，而且有時候我們無法及時接受治療來拯救我們自己。有時候牛奶或大量的水能夠稀釋掉毒素在我們血管中的濃度。我們的血管對我們來說是非常重要的，因為它攜帶了氧氣、二氧化碳和許多重要氣體。如果血管受到阻擋或含有毒素的話，他們就不能夠正常運作。所以為了我們自己的健康著想，別吃不知名的植物，特別是顏色光亮且鮮豔的植物。而且如果你在樹林中要小心任何有害的昆蟲，否則，你可能會發現你自己身陷急診室等著醫生從你的血管中移除那些毒素。

In describing toxins, the professor mentions that toxins can damage our body tissues. If our body tissues are harmed, it's likely that our body cannot function properly. Renal failure is one of the symptoms caused by toxins. Our body will be experiencing organ dysfunction. Our body still needs other chemicals, such as certain antibiotics so that our body can function well after those toxins are in our blood vessels. Sometimes milk or a large amount of water can dilute the concentration of the toxins in our blood vessels. Finally, we should be more vigilant if we are in the woods so that we can protect us from getting stung by harmful insects or consume some poisonous plants.

在描述毒素時，教授提到毒素能夠損害我們的身體組織。如果我們的身體受到損害，很可能我們的身體無法正常運作。腎衰竭是由毒素所引起的其中一個症狀之一。我們的身體會經歷器官功能不全。我們的身體仍需要其他的化學物質，例如特定的抗體，這樣我們的身體才能夠在那些毒素入侵到我們血管後良好運作。有時候牛奶或大量的水能夠稀釋在我們血管中毒素的濃度。最後，我們應該要更警惕，如果我們身處樹林中的話，這樣我們才能夠保護我們免於受到有害植物的螫咬或攝食到一些有毒的植物。

PART 01 個人喜好

PART 02 二選一話題

PART 03 概述觀點

PART 04 整合文章和講座

PART 05 討論解決辦法

PART 06 概括講座內容

整合能力強化

· 使用口說題「閱讀」原文強化「寫作」能力。

　　我們對於毒素如何能即刻殺死一個生命感到驚人。動物和植物都能產生毒素來保護自己。昆蟲會避開葉子或莖含有有害化學物質的植物，而且植物能夠避免自己本身免於被食用，所以他們可以確保自身本身的生存等等。動物，像是植物一樣有著相似的機制。有的擁有有毒的毒素所以他們能夠癱瘓或打倒獵物。儘管毒素並不是總是能發揮作用，在自然界，它可以被視為是有力的工具。

_____

_____

_____

_____

_____

_____

_____

_____

・使用口說題聽力原文練習影子跟讀，「口說」強化「聽力」能力。

We all know what toxins produced by spiders and other creatures can do to our body. Toxins damage our body tissues. Some harm our body tissues, so our body cannot function properly. Some cause organ dysfunction, such as renal failure. We cannot metabolize those toxins. That's why we need an injection of certain antibiotics or chemicals so that our body's immune system can resume working. Some toxins are too powerful, and sometimes we cannot get the treatment in time to save ourselves. Sometimes milk or a large amount of water can dilute the concentration of the toxins in our blood vessels. Our blood vessels are very important to us since they carry oxygen, carbon dioxide, and many important gases. If the blood vessels are blocked or contain toxins, they are not able to function properly. So for your own health, do not eat unknown plants, especially plants with bright, colorful colors. And beware of any harmful insects, if you are out in the woods, otherwise, you might find yourself in the emergency room waiting for the doctor to remove those toxins from your blood vessels.

· 使用口說題參考答案強化「口譯」和「口說」能力。

　　在描述毒素時，教授提到毒素能夠損害我們的身體組織。如果我們的身體受到損害，很可能我們的身體無法正常運作。腎衰竭是由毒素所引起的其中一個症狀之一。我們的身體會經歷器官功能不全。我們的身體仍需要其他的化學物質，例如特定的抗體，這樣我們的身體才能夠在那些毒素入侵到我們血管後良好運作。有時候牛奶或大量的水能夠稀釋在我們血管中毒素的濃度。最後，我們應該要更警惕，如果我們身處樹林中的話，這樣我們才能夠保護我們免於受到有害植物的螫咬或攝食到一些有毒的植物。

PART 01 個人喜好

PART 02 二選一話題

PART 03 概述觀點

PART 04 整合文章和講座

PART 05 討論解決辦法

PART 06 概括講座內容

3 Advertisements through social networking sites

透過社交網站的廣告

Narrator: you will now read a short passage and then listen to a talk on the same academic topic. You will then be asked a question about them. After you hear the question, you will have 30 seconds to prepare your response and 60 seconds to speak.

Narrator: now read the passage about **Advertisements through social networking sites.** You will have 45 seconds to read the passage. Begin reading now.

▶ MP3 061

Reading time: 45 seconds

Advertisements through social networking sites

Advertisements are everywhere, from the billboards at the entrance of the MRT station to the portrait of the movie star at the gate of the supermarket, but nowadays advertisements are not always in a tangible form. They are existing in other platforms, such as social networking sites. They can be used as a great boost to create the effects marketers want. It's not confined to people who visit the store and happens to see the advertisement. Thousands of viewers or millions of viewers can see the advertisement through social networking sites.

PART 01 個人喜好

PART 02 二選一話題

PART 03 概述觀點

PART 04 整合文章和講座

PART 05 討論解決辦法

PART 06 概括講座內容

Narrator: now listen to part of a lecture on this topic in a business class. ▶MP3 062

_____

_____

_____

_____

_____

Explain how the example from the professor's lecture tells us what's behind the advertisements through social networking sites. ▶MP3 063

Preparation Time: 30 seconds
Response Time: 60 seconds

PART 01 個人喜好

PART 02 二選一話題

PART 03 概述觀點

PART 04 整合文章和講座

PART 05 討論解決辦法

PART 06 概括講座內容

_____

_____

_____

_____

_____

（準備期間內，試著在筆記欄頁上寫下幾個所想要描述的重點並搭配前面閱讀和所聽到的內容，做出接下來的回答。）

 閱讀文章 中譯

透過社交網站的廣告

　　廣告無所不在，從在捷運站路口的廣告刊版到在超級市場入口的電影明星畫像，但是現今，廣告不再總是實體的形式。它們存在於其他平台，例如社交網站。它們可以被用於大幅提升效益以創造行銷人員所想要的效果。這不僅僅限定於參觀店面和碰巧看到廣告者。成千或數百萬的觀看者能夠透過社交網路網站觀看到廣告。

Nowadays, behavioral changes have brought some changes to the advertisement industry. Even computers are being replaced by smartphones and the iPad or related devices. People don't have to use computers at home to view a video clip. With a smartphone in hand, people can view images or videos through a smartphone at any place and at any time. A video clip viewed by millions of viewers or large audiences can create benefit for an advertising company. More viewers mean more people will know the product. The effects of the advertisement are greater than you think. Since this brings so many benefits, many marketers grab every chance they have to boost hits or likes. More likes clicked by viewers mean more people are in favor of the idea presented in the video. With these changes, we cannot downgrade the effects of these advertisements in the mind of every individual. Everyone's mind can easily be shaped or brainwashed by those images. While we are glad that there are novel ways of creating the images or videos we love, we should also beware of every message conveyed through those social networking sites.

PART 01 個人喜好

PART 02 二選一話題

PART 03 概述觀點

PART 04 整合文章和講座

PART 05 討論解決辦法

PART 06 概括講座內容

　　現今，行為改變已經導致廣告行業的一些改變。甚至電腦被智慧型手機和iPad或是相關的裝置取代。人們不需要在家裡使用電腦觀看一個視頻。有著一隻智慧型手機在手，人們能夠透過智慧型手機，在任何地方或任何時間，瀏覽圖片或影像。一則由數百萬觀看者或觀眾觀看的視頻能夠替廣告公司創造利益。許多觀看者意謂著更多人知道該產品。廣告的效果比你所想得更強大。既然此舉能夠帶來許多利益，許多行銷人員抓住每個他們能夠提高點擊率或讚的機會。更多由觀看者點的讚意謂著更多人贊同視頻裡所呈現的想法。隨著這些改變，我們不能低估這些廣告對每個人心中所產生的影響。每個人的心理能夠輕易地被那些圖像形塑或洗腦。雖然我們很高興有了更新奇的方式來創造我們喜愛的圖片或視頻，我們也應該要小心每個透過社交網站所要傳達的訊息。

In describing the advertisements through social networking sites, the professor points out the behavioral changes for consumers. We can see the message advertisements are trying to convey at any places, if we have a smartphone in our hands. Advertisement companies are welcoming these changes. The number of viewers can accumulate in an instant. In a second, the purpose of the advertisement can be reached, so marketers are grasping every chance to boost the likes through social networking sites. However, as a consumer, we should be keenly aware of what's behind the advertisement so that we will not be brainwashed.

在描述透過社交網站廣告，教授指出了對於消費者來說的行為改變。我們可以在任何地方看到廣告訊息的傳達，如果我們有智慧型手機在手。廣告公司很歡迎這樣的改變。觀看者數量能夠在片刻累積。一下子，廣告的目的就能達到，所以行銷人員抓住每個機會，透過社交網路網站提高讚的數量。然而，作為一個消費者，我們應該要敏銳地察覺出廣告背後的意圖，這樣我們就能免於被洗腦。

整合能力強化

．使用口說題「閱讀」原文強化「寫作」能力。

廣告，透過社交網路網站

　　廣告無所不在，從在捷運站路口的廣告刊版到在超級市場入口的電影明星畫像，但是現今，廣告不再總是實體的形式。它們存在於其他平台，例如社交網站。它們可以被用於大幅提升效益以創造行銷人員所想要的效果。這不僅僅限定於參觀店面和碰巧看到廣告者。成千或數百萬的觀看者能夠透過社交網路網站觀看到廣告。

PART 01 個人喜好

PART 02 二選一話題

PART 03 概述觀點

PART 04 整合文章和講座

PART 05 討論解決辦法

PART 06 概括講座內容

・使用口說題聽力原文練習影子跟讀，「口說」強化「聽力」能力。

Nowadays, behavioral changes have brought some changes to the advertisement industry. Even computers are being replaced by smartphones and the iPad or related devices. People don't have to use computers at home to view a video clip. With a smartphone in hand, people can view images or videos through a smartphone at any place and at any time. A video clip viewed by millions of viewers or large audiences can create benefit for an advertising company. More viewers mean more people will know the product. The effects of the advertisement are greater than you think. Since this brings so many benefits, many marketers grab every chance they have to boost hits or likes. More likes clicked by viewers mean more people are in favor of the idea presented in the video. With these changes, we cannot downgrade the effects of these advertisements in the mind of every individual. Everyone's mind can easily be shaped or brainwashed by those images. While we are glad that there are novel ways of creating the images or videos we love, we should also beware of every message conveyed through those social networking sites.

・使用口說題參考答案強化「口譯」和「口說」能力。

　　在描述透過社交網站廣告，教授指出了對於消費者來說的行為改變。我們可以在任何地方看到廣告訊息的傳達，如果我們有智慧型手機在手。廣告公司很歡迎這樣的改變。觀看者數量能夠在片刻累積。一下子，廣告的目的就能達到，所以行銷人員抓住每個機會，透過社交網路網站提高讚的數量。然而，作為一個消費者，我們應該要敏銳地察覺出廣告背後的意圖，這樣我們就能免於被洗腦。

01
個人喜好

02
二選一話題

03
概述觀點

04
整合文章和講座

05
討論解決辦法

06
概括講座內容

invasive species
外來物種－福壽螺

Narrator: you will now read a short passage and then listen to a talk on the same academic topic. You will then be asked a question about them. After you hear the question, you will have 30 seconds to prepare your response and 60 seconds to speak.

Narrator: now read the passage about **invasive species.** You will have 45 seconds to read the passage. Begin reading now. ▶**MP3 065**

Reading time: 45 seconds

Invasive Species

In biology, an invasive species refers to a non-native species, a species not native to a certain place. Sometimes it is accidentally introduced by humans through air travel. Other time, it is deliberately introduced. Whatever the reasons behind the introduction, an invasive species can cause unseen damage to a certain geographical location, and the damage is beyond our control. It is quite tenacious and it can thrive in that location for quite well. Under most circumstances, they have no natural enemies in the location.

PART 01 個人喜好

PART 02 二選一話題

PART 03 概述觀點

PART 04 整合文章和講座

PART 05 討論解決辦法

PART 06 概括講座內容

Narrator: now listen to part of a lecture on this topic in a biology class. ▶MP3 066

 筆記

_____

_____

_____

_____

_____

_____

口說 回答

Explain how the example from the professor's lecture tells us more about the non-native species.
▶MP3 067

Preparation Time: 30 seconds
Response Time: 60 seconds

PART 01 個人喜好

PART 02 二選一話題

PART 03 概述觀點

PART 04 整合文章和講座

PART 05 討論解決辦法

PART 06 概括講座內容

_____

_____

_____

_____

_____

_____

（準備期間內，試著在筆記欄頁上寫下幾個所想要描述的重點並搭配前面閱讀和所聽到的內容，做出接下來的回答。）

閱讀文章 中譯

　　在生物學中，外來種指的是非本土的物種，不是原產於本地的物種。有時候會不經意由人們透過航空旅行引進。在其他時候，是有意地引進。不論引進背後的原因為何，外來種能導致特定地域未能輕易被察覺的損害，而這損害是超過我們所能控制的。這物種是相當頑強的而且能夠在那個地方繁盛起來。在大多數的情況下，它們在該地區沒有天敵。

Non-native or as we call them non-indigenous species are hard to get rid of since they do not have natural enemies. Golden apple snails are a well-known non-indigenous species in Taiwan. They possess traits of non-native species, such as fast growth and rapid reproduction. They are omnivores and tend to eat the tender parts of plants, such as the stems and leaves. They are doing quite a lot of damage to rice fields and potatoes by the river bank. Harvests of agricultural crops are heavily influenced by the presence of the golden apple snails. Other Asian countries have also suffered from the harm caused by the golden apple snails. Luckily, people have come up with ways to cope with overpopulation of the golden apple snails. Fish have been used as a way to combat the golden apple snail invasion, although not as useful as fresh-water turtles. Several species of turtles can be more effective in controlling the population of golden apple snails. What's more interesting is that ducks can be used for controlling the species. Another less well-known species, the African sacred ibis also can be used to decrease the number of the species. The funny thing is they are non-native species as well. It's like using non-native species to control another non-indigenous species.

PART 01　個人喜好

PART 02　二選一話題

PART 03　概述觀點

PART 04　整合文章和講座

PART 05　討論解決辦法

PART 06　概括講座內容

　　非本土的物種或者是我們所稱的非原生的物種很難移除，因為它們沒有天敵。金蘋果蝸牛在台灣一直是因非原生種而聞名。它們擁有非本土物種的特質，例如快速生長和快速繁衍。它們是雜食性動物，而且傾向食用植物柔嫩部位，例如莖和葉子。它們對於稻田和河岸邊的馬鈴薯造成了相當的損害。農作物的收成大幅地受到金蘋果蝸牛的影響。其他亞洲國家也遭受到金蘋果蝸牛的危害。幸運地是，人們已經想出處理金蘋果蝸牛的過度成長問題。魚類已經用於對抗金蘋果蝸牛的入侵，儘管沒有比淺水水域的烏龜有效。有些烏龜能夠有效的控制金蘋果蝸牛的族群。更令人感到有趣地是鴨子也能用於控制這個物種。另一個較不知名的物種，非洲聖鸛也能用於降低這個物種的數量。有趣的是它們也不是本土物種。這像是使用非本土物種去控制另一個非原生物種。

In describing the non-native species, the professor uses a more well-known species to explain the concept. Golden apple snails have been a more well-known non-native species to us since high school, and are the non-native species here in Taiwan. Throughout the entire lecture, we can easily grasp two major traits of non-native species, fast growth and rapid reproduction. Golden apple snails possess those and they are causing quite a damage to agricultural crops, even in some Asian countries. Luckily, people have come up with ways to use other species to control the overpopulation of the golden apple snails. Species, such as fish, turtles, and even ducks, and non-native species, African sacred ibis.

在描述非本土物種時，教授使用了較知名的物種去解釋這個概念。金蘋果蝸牛一直是自從高中後，較知名的非本土物種，而且在台灣也是非本土物種。透過整個講課，我們可以輕易地掌握兩個主要的非本土物種的特徵，快速生長和快速繁殖。金蘋果蝸牛擁有那些而且它們導致農作物相當程度的危害，甚至是在一些亞洲國家。幸運地是，人們已經想出方法，使用其他物種來控制金蘋果蝸牛的族群過度成長。物種，例如魚類、烏龜和甚至是鴨子和非本土物種，非洲聖䴉。

整合能力強化

‧使用口說題「閱讀」原文強化「寫作」能力。

在生物學中，外來種指的是非本土的物種，不是原產於本地的物種。有時候會不經意由人們透過航空旅行引進。在其他時候，是有意地引進。不論引進背後的原因為何，外來種能導致特定地域未能輕易被察覺的損害，而這損害是超過我們所能控制的。這物種是相當頑強的而且能夠在那個地方繁盛起來。在大多數的情況下，它們在該地區沒有天敵。

PART 01 個人喜好

PART 02 二選一話題

PART 03 概述觀點

PART 04 整合文章和講座

PART 05 討論解決辦法

PART 06 概括講座內容

· 使用口說題聽力原文練習影子跟讀，「口說」強化「聽力」能力。

Non-native or as we call them non-indigenous species are hard to get rid of since they do not have natural enemies. Golden apple snails are a well-known non-indigenous species in Taiwan. They possess traits of non-native species, such as fast growth and rapid reproduction. They are omnivores and tend to eat the tender parts of plants, such as the stems and leaves. They are doing quite a lot of damage to rice fields and potatoes by the river bank. Harvests of agricultural crops are heavily influenced by the presence of the golden apple snails. Other Asian countries have also suffered from the harm caused by the golden apple snails. Luckily, people have come up with ways to cope with overpopulation of the golden apple snails. Fish have been used as a way to combat the golden apple snail invasion, although not as useful as fresh-water turtles. Several species of turtles can be more effective in controlling the population of golden apple snails. What's more interesting is that ducks can be used for controlling the species. Another less well-known species, the African sacred ibis also can be used to decrease the number of the species. The funny thing is they are non-native species as well. It's like using non-native species to control another non-indigenous species.

・使用口說題參考答案強化「口譯」和「口說」能力。

在描述非本土物種時，教授使用了較知名的物種去解釋這個概念。金蘋果蝸牛一直是自從高中後，較知名的非本土物種，而且在台灣也是非本土物種。透過整個講課，我們可以輕易地掌握兩個主要的非本土物種的特徵，快速生長和快速繁殖。金蘋果蝸牛擁有那些而且它們導致農作物相當程度的危害，甚至是在一些亞洲國家。幸運地是，人們已經想出方法，使用其他物種來控制金蘋果蝸牛的族群過度成長。物種，例如魚類、烏龜和甚至是鴨子和非本土物種，非洲聖䴉。

PART 01 個人喜好

PART 02 二選一話題

PART 03 概述觀點

PART 04 整合文章和講座

PART 05 討論解決辦法

PART 06 概括講座內容

5 handedness
用手習慣

Narrator: you will now read a short passage and then listen to a talk on the same academic topic. You will then be asked a question about them. After you hear the question, you will have 30 seconds to prepare your response and 60 seconds to speak.

Narrator: now read the passage about handedness. You will have 45 seconds to read the passage. Begin reading now. ▶**MP3 069**

Reading time: 45 seconds

handedness

From the moment we are born, we are gradually or eventually develop to have a preference for using right or left hands. It has been known as handedness as we know today. We are certainly more inclined to or stick to use a particular hand, either right or left to perform the task, such as writing a paper or drawing a portrait. It's relatively unlikely for one person to consecutively use right and left hands to complete a huge painting. In the work of Jing Yong, some characters are experiencing some changes and they are able to use both hands to combat villains.

PART 01 個人喜好

PART 02 二選一話題

PART 03 概述觀點

04 整合文章和講座

PART 05 討論解決辦法

PART 06 概括講座內容

Narrator: now listen to part of a lecture on this topic in a neurology class. ▶MP3 070

 筆記

_____

_____

_____

_____

_____

_____

_____

口說 回答

Explain how the example from the professor's lecture
▶MP3 071

Preparation Time: 30 seconds
Response Time: 60 seconds

PART

01

個人喜好

PART

02

二選一話題

PART

03

概述觀點

PART

04

整合文章和講座

PART

05

討論解決辦法

PART

06

概括講座內容

（準備期間內，試著在筆記欄頁上寫下幾個所想要描述的重點
並搭配前面閱讀和所聽到的內容，做出接下來的回答。）

用手習慣

　　從我們出生的時候，我們逐漸或最終發展出對於是用右手
或左手有偏好。用手習慣就如同我們現今所知道的一樣。我們
確實更傾向或著堅持使用特定的手，右手或左手來執行任務，
例如寫篇報告或繪製人物圖像。這對於一個人接續使用右手和
左手來完成一幅巨型繪圖是相對不可能的。在金庸的作品中，
有些角色經歷了一些改變，而他們能夠使用雙手來打擊惡棍。

In Jing Yong's martial arts world, we can find his in-depth look into inner parts of the characters as well as something intriguing. Handedness is one of them. Chou Bao Tung is known as a person who can use both hands in a fight with villains. He developed this skill during his solitary life on Tao Hua Dao, an island of beauty in the fiction. He teaches Guo Jing in the cave and then Xiaolongnu. Chou teaches Xiaolongnu when they are at a very critical moment. He simply askes her to use one hand to draw a square and with the other, a circle. Do it at the same time. Xiaolongnu can do it with such an ease. Performing her martial arts skills, Maiden Heart Sutra, by using both her hands to double her ability. The elevation of the skills can save her at such an emergent moment. Their enemy, the Golden Wheel Lama, is surprised to find that she can use both hands to perform martial arts skills. It's such a prefect blend of the plot and hand dominance all in one.

PART 01 個人喜好
PART 02 二選一話題
PART 03 概述觀點
PART 04 整合文章和講座
PART 05 討論解決辦法
PART 06 概括講座內容

在金庸的武俠世界中，我們可以發現他深入的討論到角色的內心以及一些令人感到有趣的部分。用手習慣即是其中一項。周伯通一直以能使用雙手來與惡棍對戰聞名。他發展了這樣的武功是在他獨居於桃花島時，小説中的美麗島嶼。他在洞穴中教導郭靖然後是小龍女。周教導小龍女當他們處於非常緊急的時刻。他簡單地要求她使用一隻手畫方，另一隻手畫圓。同時做這個動作。小龍女可以很輕易地做這個動作。藉由使用雙手展現她的武功，玉女心經，使她展示出的武功效果倍增。武功能力的提升在危急的時候救了她。他們的敵人，金輪法王，很驚訝地發現她能使用雙手來展現武功。這即是情節和手的支配性的完美結合。

Handedness is such an intriguing topic to most of us. In describing the handedness, the professor uses the example of the eastern fiction, the work of Jing Yong to explain the concept. Although we are stick to a certain hand to do things, using another hands or using both hands to do things can have amazing outcomes. In the fiction, the confinement in the cave has led to an invention of using both hands to perform the martial arts skills. Later accounts of the fiction, heroine, Xiaolongnu begins to learn this skills by first using one hand to paint a square and another a circle. With her ability doubled, she can eventually beat the villain, the Golden Wheel Lama. We certainly cannot limit ourselves by the hand dominance.

對我們大多數的人來說，用手習慣是如此令人感到有趣的話題。在描述用手習慣時，教授使用了東方小說中的例子，金庸的作品來解釋這個概念。儘管我們堅定地使用特定的手來做事情，使用另一隻手或使用雙手來做事能夠有驚人的結果。在小說中，監禁於洞穴中導致發明了使用雙手來展示武功的方法。在小說後的描述中，小龍女開始學習這個武功是藉由一手畫方，而另一隻手畫圓。隨著她的能力倍增，她能夠最終打敗惡棍，金輪法王。我們確實不能因為手的支配性而為自己設限。

PART 01 個人喜好

PART 02 二選一話題

PART 03 概述觀點

PART 04 整合文章和講座

PART 05 討論解決辦法

PART 06 概括講座內容

整合能力強化

・使用口說題「閱讀」原文強化「寫作」能力。

用手習慣

　　從我們出生的時候，我們逐漸或最終發展出對於是用右手或左手有偏好。用手習慣就如同我們現今所知道的一樣。我們確實更傾向或著堅持使用特定的手，右手或左手來執行任務，例如寫篇報告或繪製人物圖像。這對於一個人接續使用右手和左手來完成一幅巨型繪圖是相對性不可能的。在金庸的作品中，有些角色經歷了一些改變，而他們能夠使用雙手來打擊惡棍。

_____

_____

_____

_____

_____

_____

_____

_____

· 使用口說題聽力原文練習影子跟讀，「口說」強化「聽力」能力。

In Jing Yong's martial arts world, we can find his in-depth look into inner parts of the characters as well as something intriguing. Handedness is one of them. Chou Bao Tung is known as a person who can use both hands to in a flight with villains. He developed this skill during his solitary life on Tao Hua Dao, an island of beauty in the fiction. He teaches Guo Jing in the cave and then Xiaolongnu. Chou teaches Xiaolongnu when they at a very critical moment. He simply askes her to use one hand to draw a square and the other, a circle. Do it at the same time. Xiaolongnu can do it with such ease. Performing her martial arts skills, Maiden Heart Sutra, by using both her hands to double her ability. The elevation of the skills can save her at such an emergent moment. Their enemy, the Golden Wheel Lama, is surprised to find that she can use both hands to perform martial arts skills. It's such a prefect blend of the plot and hand dominance all in one.

‧使用口說題參考答案強化「口譯」和「口說」能力。

　　對我們大多數的人來說，用手習慣是如此令人感到有趣的話題。在描述用手習慣時，教授使用了東方小說中的例子，金庸的作品來解釋這個概念。儘管我們堅定地使用特定的手來做事情，使用另一隻手或使用雙手來做事能夠有驚人的結果。在小說中，監禁於洞穴中導致發明了使用雙手來展示武功的方法。在小說後的描述中，小龍女開始學習這個武功是藉由一手畫方，而另一隻手畫圓。隨著她的能力倍增，她能夠最終打敗惡棍，金輪法王。我們確實不能因為手的支配性而為自己設限。

PART 01 個人喜好

PART 02 二選一話題

PART 03 概述觀點

PART 04 整合文章和講座

PART 05 討論解決辦法

PART 06 概括講座內容

natural enemy
天敵

Narrator: you will now read a short passage and then listen to a talk on the same academic topic. You will then be asked a question about them. After you hear the question, you will have 30 seconds to prepare your response and 60 seconds to speak.

Narrator: now read the passage about **natural enemy.** You will have 45 seconds to read the passage. Begin reading now. ▶**MP3 073**

Reading time: 45 seconds

Natural Enemy

In biology, predators feed on their prey. All creatures have their own natural enemy, except for a relative few which is in the top of the pyramid. Species at the top of the food chain has none or little enemies. Natural enemies are a very good mechanism in biology to maintain the species within the regulated amount. Species without natural enemies will lead to overpopulation and this would cause a great interference or damage to the environment.

PART 01 個人喜好

PART 02 二選一話題

PART 03 概述觀點

PART 04 整合文章和講座

PART 05 討論解決辦法

PART 06 概括講座內容

Narrator: now listen to part of a lecture on this topic in a biology class. ▶ MP3 074

 筆記

_____

_____

_____

_____

_____

_____

口說 回答

Explain how the example from the professor's lecture tells us more about the function of the natural enemy. ▶ MP3 075

Preparation Time: 30 seconds
Response Time: 60 seconds

_____

_____

_____

_____

_____

_____

_____

（準備期間內，試著在筆記欄頁上寫下幾個所想要描述的重點並搭配前面閱讀和所聽到的內容，做出接下來的回答。）

👁 **閱讀文章 中譯**

　　在生物學中，捕食者以他們的獵物為食。所有生物都有它們的天敵除了一些少數在食物金字塔頂端的物種。在食物鏈頂端的物種幾乎沒有敵人。天敵在生物學中有著非常好的機制，能維持物種在規定性的量裡。物種沒有天敵的話會導致族群過剩，這會導致對環境很大的干擾或對環境的損害。

In biology, we have witnessed lots of videos about the relationships among species. No matter how powerful they are or how many weapons or armor they are equipped with, a lot of species have their own natural enemy. Crabs have great armor, but they are susceptible to attack by octopuses and eels. Scorpions may possess a powerful toxin, but they are the meal of some mammals. The toxin poses no threat to those mammals. Spiders may have poisonous fangs, but they are the prey for some birds. Birds eat spiders of all sizes. Monkeys are also the natural enemy of spiders.

Predators are always out there looking for food. Victory in the natural world often only lasts for seconds. We should be glad that there are natural enemies out there doing their job; otherwise, we would live in a world where some species overpopulate it and cause considerable damage to the place we live. Another great thing about natural enemies is that they can act as a powerful tool for the control of certain species without causing harm to the environment.

　　在生物學，我們已經目睹了許多視頻是關於物種間的關係。不論他們多麼強大或配有許多武器或裝甲，許多物種有它們的天敵。螃蟹有著強大的裝甲，但是它們易於受到章魚和鰻魚的攻擊。毒蠍可能擁有強大的毒素，但是它們是其他哺乳類動物的餐點。毒素對於那些哺乳類動物無威脅。蜘蛛可能有著毒牙，但它們是有些鳥類的獵物。鳥類吃各種大小的蜘蛛。猴子也是蜘蛛的天敵。

　　掠食者總是在外頭找尋食物。在自然界中，勝利通常僅持續幾秒鐘。我們應該要高興，掠食者在外頭執行他們該做的事。否則，我們會活在一個某些物種過度繁殖的世界裡，這會對於我們所居住的地方造成相當程度的損害。天敵另一個偉大之處是，他們可以充當控制特定物種的強大工具，而卻不會對環境造成損害。

In describing the concept of natural enemy, the professor lists several species. They are acting as examples of animals which possess weapons or armors, but they are not invincible. They have natural enemies, too. Crabs, scorpions, spiders, and so on. Natural enemies have the resistance to the toxin or the weapon they possess. Natural predators are doing there job all day finding their own meals, and they are maintaining certain population in a specific number. Overpopulations of a certain species can cause problems to the place we live. Another function of the natural enemies is that they can be used to control certain species without doing damage to the environment.

在描述天敵的概念時，教授列出了幾個物種。它們充當了具有武器或裝甲物種的例子，但它們並非無堅不摧。它們也有著天敵。螃蟹、毒蠍、蜘蛛等等的。天敵對於那些物種所持有的毒液或武器有抵抗力。天敵只是完成它們整天的工作，找尋它們的餐點，而且它們有著維持了特定族群在特定數量的功用。特定物種的族群過剩能導致我們生活地方出現問題。另一個天敵的功用是它們可以被用於控制特定物種的數量而不會造成環境的損害。

整合能力強化

・使用口說題「閱讀」原文強化「寫作」能力。

　　在生物學中，捕食者以他們的獵物為食。所有生物都有它們的天敵除了一些少數在食物金字塔頂端的物種。在食物鏈頂端的物種幾乎沒有敵人。天敵在生物學中有著非常好的機制，能維持物種在規定性的量裡。物種沒有天敵的話會導致族群過剩，這會導致對環境很大的干擾或對環境的損害。

PART 01 個人喜好

PART 02 二選一話題

PART 03 概述觀點

PART 04 整合文章和講座

PART 05 討論解決辦法

PART 06 概括講座內容

・使用口說題聽力原文練習影子跟讀，「口說」強化「聽力」能力。

In biology, we have witnessed lots of videos about the relationships among species. No matter how powerful they are or how many weapons or armor they are equipped with, a lot of species have their own natural enemy. Crabs have great armor, but they are susceptible to attack by octopuses and eels. Scorpions may possess a powerful toxin, but they are the meal of some mammals. The toxin poses no threat to those mammals. Spiders may have poisonous fangs, but they are the prey for some birds. Birds eat spiders of all sizes. Monkeys are also the natural enemy of spiders.

Predators are always out there looking for food. Victory in the natural world often only lasts for seconds. We should be glad that there are natural enemies out there doing their job; otherwise, we would live in a world where some species overpopulate it and cause considerable damage to the place we live. Another great thing about natural enemies is that they can act as a powerful tool for the control of certain species without causing harm to the environment.

・**使用口說題參考答案強化「口譯」和「口說」能力。**

　　在描述天敵的概念，教授列出了幾個物種。它們充當了具有武器或裝甲物種的例子，但它們並非無堅不摧。它們也有著天敵。螃蟹、毒蠍、蜘蛛等等的。天敵對於那些物種所持有的毒液或武器有抵抗力。天敵只是完成它們整天的工作，找尋它們的餐點，而且它們有著維持了特定族群在特定數量的功用。特定物種的族群過剩能導致我們生活地方出現問題。另一個天敵的功用是它們可以被用於控制特定物種的數量而不會造成環境的損害。

PART 01 個人喜好

PART 02 二選一話題

PART 03 概述觀點

PART 04 整合文章和講座

PART 05 討論解決辦法

PART 06 概括講座內容

part 5

討論解決
辦法題

討論解決辦法題則選擇了六個常見
的主題，這個 part 的主要得分關
鍵在於掌握聽一段對話後，能摘要
並口述，對於有常在看影集的考生
是非常容易的，甚至不太用準備。
多數考生可能太適應聽一段訊息
後，回答選擇題的題型，例如新多
益等等，可以使用這個單元的其他
設計，像是跟讀及默寫一段聽力，
強化自己聽到訊息的精確度！（部
分外文系聽力課程其實還是有相對
要求學生要默寫出聽到一定訊息量
的話，這個練習對聽力的進步其實
蠻有效的。）

1

Scheduling conflict
時程安排的衝突

Narrator: Your will now listen to a conversation. You will then be asked a question about it. After you hear the question, you will have 20 seconds to prepare your response and 60 seconds to speak.

Narrator: now listen to two students discussing possible solutions. ▶**MP3 077**

Question 1

Briefly summarize the problem and two possible solutions. Then state which solution you recommend and explain why.

Preparation time: 20s
Response time: 60s

☆ 筆記

_____

_____

_____

_____

_____

_____

_____

（試著寫下聽到的訊息，並確定自己掌握了重要的主旨，以便於回答摘要題所提到的討論內容。）

Jack: you seem worried? What's going on?

Cindy: I think I have a scheduling conflict. My third interview at ABC Airline and my final exam are on the same date…it's quite unlikely that I can do both of them in one day…and I don't want to lose the chance to interview with ABC Airline…

Jack: why don't you tell your professor and reschedule the date for your final…

Cindy: what if the professor says "NO"?

Jack: then you have to take the risk…take the taxi right after the interview…to see if you can make it back in time…

Cindy: that's certainly the most wild and adventurous thing I've ever heard…

傑克： 妳看起來有點擔心？發生了什麼事嗎？

辛蒂： 我覺得我有時程衝突的問題。我在ABC航空公司的第三回合面試和我的期末考是在同一天...要在同天內完成這兩件事幾乎不可能...而且我不想要失去ABC航空公司的面試機會...。

傑克： 為什麼不告訴妳的教授然後重新安排妳的期末考試呢...。

辛蒂： 萬一教授説「不能」呢？

傑克： 那麼妳必須要冒個險...在面試結束後搭乘計程車...看是否能及時趕回來...。

辛蒂： 這確實是我聽過最瘋狂和冒險的事...。

PART 01 個人喜好

PART 02 二選一話題

PART 03 概述觀點

PART 04 整合文章和講座

PART 05 討論解決辦法

PART 06 概括講座內容

The woman is having a scheduling conflict. Her interview at ABC Airline and her final exam are on the same date. There are two possible solutions in the conversation. The first solution is that she can talk to the professor to see if she can take the test on another day. The second solution is risky. She can take a taxi right after the interview. I would recommend the second solution because I have a very similar experience before, and normally professors are willing to arrange another day for you. And imagine how hard it is to eventually go to the third round. The second solution is too risky, so I won't recommend the second one. You can blow either one.

女子有時程衝突的問題。她在ABC航空公司的面試和她的期末考試在同一天。在會話中有兩個可能的解決方案。第一個解決方案是她可以與教授談談,看是否能讓她在其他天考試。第二個解決方案是有風險的。她可以在面試後搭計程車。我會建議第二個解決方案因為我之前有過非常相同的經驗,而通常教授會願意替妳安排另一天考試。而且很難想像要多努力才能進到第三輪的面試。第二個解決方案太冒險了,所以我不會建議第二個解決方案。妳會搞砸其中一件事。

◇ 整合能力強化

· 重新聽一次對話並將內容默寫出來。　　▶MP3 077

PART 01 個人喜好

PART 02 二選一話題

PART 03 概述觀點

PART 04 整合文章和講座

PART 05 討論解決辦法

PART 06 概括講座內容

2 Student ID card
忘記帶學生證

Narrator: Your will now listen to a conversation. You will then be asked a question about it. After you hear the question, you will have 20 seconds to prepare your response and 60 seconds to speak.

Narrator: now listen to two students discussing possible solutions. ▶**MP3 079**

Question 2

Briefly summarize the problem and two possible solutions. Then state which solution you recommend and explain why.

Preparation time: 20s
Response time: 60s

⭐ 筆記

_____

_____

_____

_____

_____

_____

（試著寫下聽到的訊息，並確定自己掌握了重要的主旨，以便於回答摘要題所提到的討論內容。）

PART 01 個人喜好

PART 02 二選一話題

PART 03 概述觀點

PART 04 整合文章和講座

PART 05 討論解決辦法

PART 06 概括講座內容

Mary: oh my god⋯what an idiot⋯I forgot to bring my student ID card⋯I need that so that I can get into the library⋯

Jack: what about using my student ID card⋯I can rush back to the dorm and get it for you⋯

Mary: but 20 minutes⋯if you're running from here to the dorm⋯are you sure⋯going back and forth will take you 40 minutes⋯.

Jack: here is another idea⋯⋯just follow another student and there seems to be a 5 second gap after the previous person uses the student ID card⋯you can definitely go in there before the door closes⋯

Mary: what a brilliant idea⋯thanks⋯

瑪莉： 我的天啊!...真是白癡...我忘記帶我的學生證了...我需要學生證這樣我才能進到圖書館裡頭...。

傑克： 要使用我的學生證嗎...我可以衝回宿舍然後拿給妳...。

瑪莉： 但是20分鐘的時間...如果你從這裡跑回宿舍的話...你確定嗎？...來回這樣的畫要花你40分鐘的時間...。

傑克： 我有另一個想法...跟著另一個學生後頭而且在前一個學生使用學生證後，似乎有5秒的間隔空檔...你可以在門關閉前就進到裡頭了...。

瑪莉： 真是個聰明的想法...謝謝囉...。

The woman is having a problem for not bringing her student ID. The man offers two possible solutions in the conversation. He is so kind that he is willing to go back to the dorm to get his student ID for her. The second solution is pretty easy. You go right behind your classmates or the person who just entered the library. If I had a slightest feeling for the guy, I would recommend the first solution. Let the guy do the things or errands for you. If not, choosing the second solution will definitely make things easier.

女子似乎有著問題，因為她忘記攜帶她的學生證了。在對話中，男子提供了兩個可能的解決方案。他很善良的說他願意往返宿舍將自己的學生證給她。第二個解決方案是相當容易的。你只要跟在你同學的後面或剛進圖書館的人後頭即可。如果你對於男子有些微感覺的話，我會建議你選擇第一個解決方案。讓那個男子作些事或替你做些差事。如果不是的話選擇第二個解決方案會讓事情更容易進行些。

整合能力強化　▶MP3 079

・重新聽力一次對話並將內容默寫出來。

PART 01 個人喜好

PART 02 二選一話題

PART 03 概述觀點

PART 04 整合文章和講座

PART 05 討論解決辦法

PART 06 概括講座內容

3

Wanna Saving Some Money

搬家—但又想省搬家費用

Narrator: Your will now listen to a conversation. You will then be asked a question about it. After you hear the question, you will have 20 seconds to prepare your response and 60 seconds to speak.

Narrator: now listen to two students discussing possible solutions. ▶**MP3 081**

Question 3

Briefly summarize the problem and two possible solutions. Then state which solution you recommend and explain why.

Preparation time: 20s
Response time: 60s

☆ 筆記

_____

_____

_____

_____

_____

_____

_____

_____

（試著寫下聽到的訊息，並確定自己掌握了重要的主旨，以便於回答摘要題所提到的討論內容。）

PART 01 個人喜好

PART 02 二選一話題

PART 03 概述觀點

PART 04 整合文章和講座

PART 05 討論解決辦法

PART 06 概括講座內容

Mary: I heard you are moving…so where is the moving van…I'd like to take a photo to make it look like I'm moving after all…

Cindy: I'm not calling a moving service…it's too expensive…

Mary: perhaps I can help…I know several guys from the fire station…and I'm sure they would love to help you…since you look pretty lovely…

Cindy: wow…are you sure they can do that for me…

Mary: pretty…sure…if they cannot come…there is another alternative…I know someone who works as a truck driver part-time…I can call him, too…

Cindy: that's fantastic…I should probably take you out to dinner after the whole moving thing is over…

瑪莉：　我聽説你要搬家了...所以搬家貨車在哪呢？...我想要拍照，這樣可以看起來好像是我要搬家...。

辛蒂：　我沒有要叫搬家服務...它太貴了...。

瑪莉：　或許我可以幫忙...我知道消防隊的幾個男子...而且我確信他們會很願意幫妳忙...妳看起來很可人。

辛蒂：　哇!...妳確定他們會願意這樣幫我嗎？

瑪莉：　相當...確定...如果他們不來的話...有另一個替代方案...我知道一個兼職開卡車的人...我也可以呼叫他...。

辛蒂：　這樣太棒了...我應該可能要帶妳去吃個晚餐，在整個搬家事情都結束之後。

PART 01 個人喜好

PART 02 二選一話題

PART 03 概述觀點

PART 04 整合文章和講座

PART 05 討論解決辦法

PART 06 概括講座內容

The woman in the conversation has a problem. She wants to save money by not calling a moving service. The other woman in the conversation offers her two possible solutions. The first one is to call the firefighters she knows to have them help her move the furniture and they can save her money. The second solution also involves asking other people for help. Another friend who is a truck driver. I would recommend the first one because I'm a people person. I enjoy meeting different people and getting to know them a bit. It's kind of cool that you get to have firefighters to help you move furniture, and you can get to know them afterwards.

對話中的女子有個問題。 她想要省錢而不叫搬家服務。另一位對話中的女子提供了兩個可能的解決方案。第一個是叫她認識的消防員來幫忙他們搬家具，這樣他們可以省錢。第二個解決方案也包含叫其他人來幫忙。另一個朋友是卡車司機。我會建議第一個解決方案因為我是愛交朋友的人。我喜愛與其他人碰面，然後認識他們一些。這很酷，你可以有消防員來幫你搬家具，而且妳可以在之後認識他們。

◆ 整合能力強化   ▶MP3 081

・重新聽力一次對話並將內容默寫出來。

_____

_____

_____

_____

_____

_____

_____

_____

_____

_____

_____

_____

PART 01 個人喜好

PART 02 二選一話題

PART 03 概述觀點

PART 04 整合文章和講座

PART 05 討論解決辦法

PART 06 概括講座內容

Not Having Enough Time

健身—健身的時間不夠

Narrator: Your will now listen to a conversation. You will then be asked a question about it. After you hear the question, you will have 20 seconds to prepare your response and 60 seconds to speak.

Narrator: now listen to two students discussing possible solutions. ▶**MP3 083**

Question 4

Briefly summarize the problem and two possible solutions. Then state which solution you recommend and explain why.

Preparation time: 20s
Response time: 60s

☆ 筆記

_____

_____

_____

_____

_____

_____

_____

（試著寫下聽到的訊息，並確定自己掌握了重要的主旨，以便於回答摘要題所提到的討論內容。）

PART 01 個人喜好

PART 02 二選一話題

PART 03 概述觀點

PART 04 整合文章和講座

PART 05 討論解決辦法

PART 06 概括講座內容

Mary: how's everything going?

Jack: I've been itching to get rid of some irrelevant things in life…so I will have more time to exercise…

Mary: exercise…meaning going to the gym?

Jack: yep…

Mary: everyone only has 24 hours a day …perhaps you should quit your part-time job…you don't even need the money…

Jack: that's a pretty good suggestion…

Mary: or…you can move closer to the school…then you don't have to spend lots of time commuting…in exchange you will have like 2 more hours per day….

Jack: that's the thought that never comes into my mind…I should think about it…perhaps that's the way out…

PART 01 個人喜好

PART 02 二選一話題

PART 03 概述觀點

PART 04 整合文章和講座

PART 05 討論解決辦法

PART 06 概括講座內容

瑪莉： 最近一切都好嗎？

傑克： 我一直想要擺脫掉一些生活中無關緊要的事情…這樣我會有更多的時間可以運動…。

瑪莉： 運動…指的是上健身房嗎？

傑克： 是的…。

瑪莉： 每個人每天只有24小時的時間…或許你應該要辭掉兼職工作…你甚至不需要金錢。

傑克： 這是相當好的建議。

瑪莉： 或…你可以搬到離學校近的地方…那麼你就不需要花費許多的通勤時間了…換來的是你會每天有多兩小時的時間…。

傑克： 這是我從沒想到的想法…我應該要思考看看…或許這是個解決辦法。

 ▶MP3 084

The man in the conversation has a problem. He wants to put irrelevant things aside so that he can have time to go to the gym. The woman in the conversation offers two possible solutions. The first one is to quit his part-time job so he will have more time. The second solution is to move closer to the school so that he does not need to commute. I will recommend the second one because commuting is such a waste of time, especially if it takes longer than an hour. Imagine an hour. How many things you can do in an hour, let alone two more hours. So definitely the second solution.

對話中的男子有個問題。他想要將無關緊要的事情擺到一旁，這樣他就能有時間上健身房了。對話中的女子提供了兩個可能的解決方案。第一個是辭掉他的兼職工作這樣一來他就有更多時間。第二的解決方案是搬到離學校近的地方，這樣一來他就不需要通勤。我會建議第二的解決方案，因為通勤是如此浪費時間的事，尤其是要花費超過一小時的通勤時間。想像一小時。有多少事情你能於一小時內完成，更別說是兩小時多了。所以一定是第二的解決方案。

💎 **整合能力強化**　▶ MP3 083

・ 重新聽力一次對話並將內容默寫出來。

PART 01 個人喜好

PART 02 二選一話題

PART 03 概述觀點

PART 04 整合文章和講座

PART 05 討論解決辦法

PART 06 概括講座內容

5

Blow Someone Off

看電影—被女伴放鴿子

Narrator: Your will now listen to a conversation. You will then be asked a question about it. After you hear the question, you will have 20 seconds to prepare your response and 60 seconds to speak.

Narrator: now listen to two students discussing possible solutions. ▶**MP3 085**

Question 5

Briefly summarize the problem and two possible solutions. Then state which solution you recommend and explain why.

Preparation time: 20s
Response time: 60s

筆記

_____

_____

_____

_____

_____

_____

_____

（試著寫下聽到的訊息，並確定自己掌握了重要的主旨，以便於回答摘要題所提到的討論內容。）

01 個人喜好

02 二選一話題

03 概述觀點

04 整合文章和講座

05 討論解決辦法

06 概括講座內容

Mark: I think my date is not coming⋯

Mary: why?

Mark: it's been ten minutes⋯I think she is not coming⋯ the movie is going to start in 10 minutes⋯

Mary: wow⋯dude⋯I don't know what to say⋯are you sure she knows the exact⋯date⋯

Mark: I texted her yesterday⋯but she didn't reply⋯

Mary: perhaps you should call her⋯to see if she plans to come⋯

Mark: yep⋯I should call her⋯

Mary: or⋯you can go with me⋯two front row seats⋯ what a waste⋯

Mark: I'm going to leave a line message to her⋯saying I'm going to see the movie with someone else⋯

馬克： 我想我的約會對象不會來了。

瑪莉： 為什麼呢？

馬克： 已經十分鐘了...我認為她不會來了...電影將於十分鐘內開播。

瑪莉： 哇!...兄弟...我不知道該說什麼...你確定她知道確切的...日期嗎...？

馬克： 我昨天傳訊息給她了...但是她沒有回覆...。

瑪莉： 或許你應該要打給她...看她是否想要來...。

馬克： 是的...我應該要打給她...。

瑪莉： 或者是...你可以跟我一起進去看...兩個首排位子...多浪費啊!...。

馬克： 我要留則line訊息給她...跟她說我會與其他人去看電影了...。

The man in the conversation has a problem. His date is not coming. The girl in the conversation offers two solutions. The first one is to call the girl to see if she is still coming to the movie. The second one is kind of selfish. She goes to the movie with the man. I will recommend he go to the movie with another woman. Because it would be such a waste. A ticket still means money spent on it. Going to the movie with another woman sounds wise, and it adds value to your friendship.

對話中的男子有個問題。他的約會對象不來了。對話中的另一個女子提供了兩個解決方案。第一個解決方案是打給那個女孩看她是否仍想要來看電影。第二個是有點自私的解決方案。她會與男子一同去看電影。我會建議他跟另一個女子去看電影。因為這會很浪費。一張票也意謂著花費了金錢在上頭。與另一位女子去看電影聽起來是明智的，而且這對友誼來說是增值的。

整合能力強化　▶MP3 085

‧ 重新聽力一次對話並將內容默寫出來。

PART 01 個人喜好

PART 02 二選一話題

PART 03 概述觀點

PART 04 整合文章和講座

PART 05 討論解決辦法

PART 06 概括講座內容

Swimsuit

游泳—忘記帶泳衣

Narrator: Your will now listen to a conversation. You will then be asked a question about it. After you hear the question, you will have 20 seconds to prepare your response and 60 seconds to speak.

Narrator: now listen to two students discussing possible solutions. ▶**MP3 087**

Question 6

Briefly summarize the problem and two possible solutions. Then state which solution you recommend and explain why.

Preparation time: 20s
Response time: 60s

筆記

_____

_____

_____

_____

_____

_____

_____

（試著寫下聽到的訊息，並確定自己掌握了重要的主旨，以便於回答摘要題所提到的討論內容。）

PART 01 個人喜好

PART 02 二選一話題

PART 03 概述觀點

PART 04 整合文章和講座

PART 05 討論解決辦法

PART 06 概括講座內容

Cindy: I forgot to bring my swim suit···

Jack: you can borrow mine···

Cindy: borrow yours···?...stop joking around···you're a guy···

Jack: haha····.alright····.perhaps you should buy one.. wearing some else's swim suit is kind of odd···

Cindy: ···it's just so not···Hy..gienic···what else can I do··· the swimming course is in ten minutes···going to be late···

Jack: telling the coach that you're not feeling well···a woman using that kind of excuse generally works···

Cindy: thanks···I can't think of a better way···I will do either one of your suggestions···

辛蒂： 我忘了帶我的游泳衣了...。

傑克： 你可以借我的...。

辛蒂： 借你的...？別再開玩笑了...你是男生...。

傑克： 哈哈...好啦...或許你應該要買件...穿別人的泳衣也有點怪怪的...。

辛蒂： 就是...很不...衛...生...我還能怎麼做呢...游泳課再十分鐘就要開始了...快要遲到了...。

傑克： 告訴教練你覺得不舒服...一個女孩用這樣的理由通常會奏效...。

辛蒂： 謝謝...我想不出更好的辦法了...我選擇你建議的其中一項建議...。

The woman in the conversation forgets to bring her swim suit to the school. The man in the conversation offers two possible solutions. The first solution is to buy a swim suit since wearing someone else's swim suit is not hygienic. The second solution is to make an excuse for not feeling well so that she does not have to worry about it. I would recommend the second solution since the first solution involves spending extra money. Plus, being a woman has some advantages. So why don't you use it so that you can temporarily get away with swimming, and the coach will not find out about it.

對話中的女子在學校忘了攜帶她的泳衣了。對話中的男子提供了兩個可能的解決辦法。第一個解決辦法是買件泳衣，既然穿別人的泳衣不是很衛生。第二個解決方案是用身體不適這個理由，這樣一來的話她就不用擔心了。我會建議第二個解決方案，因為第一個解決方案要多花錢。再説，身為一個女生有些優點。所以為什麼不好好利用呢…這樣你就可以暫時告別游泳的事，而且教練也不會發現…。

💎 整合能力強化　▶MP3 087

· 重新聽力一次對話並將內容默寫出來。

_____

_____

_____

_____

_____

_____

_____

_____

_____

_____

_____

_____

_____

_____

_____

PART 01 個人喜好
PART 02 二選一話題
PART 03 概述觀點
PART 04 整合文章和講座
PART 05 討論解決辦法
PART 06 概括講座內容

part 6

概括講座內容題

這個 part 是概括講座內容題，與 part 5 討論解決辦法題不同的是，這部分是要聆聽一個學術講座且不太可能遇到考生熟悉的主題，在聽力上會較吃力，考生要多強化練習這個主題，可以藉由書中的練習，熟悉聽一段話後摘要出重點內容後就立即大量練習官方試題。

1

camouflage

生物學：偽裝

Narrator: in this question, you will listen to part of a lecture. Then you will be asked a question about it. After the question, you will have 20 seconds to prepare and 60 seconds to respond. ▶**MP3 089**

Narrator: now listen to part of a talk in a biology class.

☆ 筆記

PART 01 個人喜好

PART 02 二選一話題

PART 03 概述觀點

PART 04 整合文章和講座

PART 05 討論解決辦法

PART 06 概括講座內容

口說 回答

Explain how the example from the professor's lecture tells us why camouflage sometimes works and sometimes doesn't. ▶MP3 090

Preparation Time: 30 seconds
Response Time: 60 seconds

_____

_____

_____

_____

_____

_____

_____

_____

（準備期間內，試著在筆記欄頁上寫下幾個所想要描述的重點並搭配前面閱讀和所聽到的內容，做出接下來的回答。）

聽力原文 和中譯

　　Today we will cover the part I've been wanting to talk about. camouflage. Camouflage is a great mechanism in the natural world. Insects, such as mantises use camouflage to make them less visible to their prey or their predators. This will greatly increase the success rate of capturing their prey. They can be found hidden underneath branches. Their leaf-like or branch-like colors help them masquerade. Other species with bright and colorful colors can be found hidden beneath flowers. When hummingbirds are approaching, they are preparing to attack. The attack can happen in such a short time that often the hummingbird is unable to avoid it.

　　今天我們會涵蓋的部分是我一直想要討論的部分。偽裝。偽裝是自然界中很棒的機制。昆蟲，例如螳螂使用偽裝來使得它們在獵物或捕食者中較不顯眼。這會大幅增加它們捕捉獵物的成功率。它們藏於樹枝下方。它們像枯葉或像樹枝顏色幫助它們偽裝。其他物種有著光亮或鮮豔的顏色能藏於花朵下方。當蜂鳥靠近時，它們會準備攻擊機會。攻擊的時間能發生於很短的時間內，通常蜂鳥無法避開掉。

PART 01 個人喜好
PART 02 二選一話題
PART 03 概述觀點
PART 04 整合文章和講座
PART 05 討論解決辦法
PART 06 概括講座內容

But camouflage will not always work. Some species have developed keen vision to counter with the camouflage. Chameleons are also known for their camouflage ability. They use coloration to camouflage themselves. Their tongue can be quite a powerful tool. It can attack insects, such as mantises in a second. The camouflage used by mantises will not work in most circumstances. Before the insect is aware of the attack, the tongue touches the body of the insect and the next time we know, they are in the mouth of the chameleon. Perhaps to the eyes of the predator, the ability to camouflage is just a way to earn yourself a few more days to live, especially when most defense mechanisms like camouflage won't work for predators. It's just some lame stunt.

但是偽裝並不總是能發揮作用。其他物種可能可以發展出很敏銳的視野來應對這樣的偽裝。變色龍以它們的偽裝能力聞名。它們使用顏色來偽裝它們自己。它們的舌頭可以是相當強大的工具。它可以攻擊昆蟲，例如螳螂，在一秒內。螳螂使用的偽裝在大多數情況下是沒辦法發揮作用的。在昆蟲能察覺出攻擊前，舌頭觸碰到昆蟲的身體上，而接下來我們知道的是他們在變色龍的嘴巴裡了。或許對於捕食者的眼中，偽裝的能力只是一個讓你自己能多活幾天的伎倆，特別是當大多數的防護機制像是偽裝對捕食者發揮不了作用的時候。這只是一些不堪一擊的伎倆。

♡ 口說參考答案 和中譯　▶MP3 091

The professor uses insects as examples to explain the concept of camouflage. Mantises use camouflage to make them invisible to their predators or prey so that they can have a high chance of survival. Some use coloration as a way to camouflage. Hummingbirds often are incapable of noticing the mantis is near them.

Other species, such as chameleons also use coloration to protect themselves. But coloration used by mantises seem of no use to them because their attack can happen so quickly before the prey is aware of that. Like what the professor says in the ending, "perhaps to the eye of the predator, the ability to camouflage is just a way to earn yourself a few more days to live, especially when most defense mechanism like camouflage won't work for predators. It's just some lame stunt."

　教授使用昆蟲作為解釋偽裝概念的例子。螳螂使用偽裝使它們在它們的捕食者眼中較不顯眼，所以它們能夠有更高的生存率。有些使用顏色作為偽裝的方式。蜂鳥通常無力察覺出螳螂靠近它們。

　其他物種，例如變色龍也使用顏色來保護它們自己。但是由螳螂所使用的顏色對變色龍來說沒有用，因為變色龍的攻擊

PART 01 個人喜好

PART 02 二選一話題

PART 03 概述觀點

PART 04 整合文章和講座

PART 05 討論解決辦法

PART 06 概括講座內容

常來的太快了，在獵物能察覺之前。像教授在結尾所説的，「偽裝的能力只是一個讓你自己能多活幾天的伎倆，特別是當大多數的防護機制像是偽裝對捕食者發揮不了作用的時候。這只是一些不堪一擊的伎倆。」

 ## 整合能力強化 ❶：口說與聽力

影子跟讀：看參考答案，並對於聽力原文做影子跟讀練習，提升主題答題並利用口說和聽力的關聯性強化聽力能力。

Today we will cover the part I've been wanting to talk about. camouflage. Camouflage is a great mechanism in the natural world. Insects, such as mantises use camouflage to make them less visible to their prey or their predators. This will greatly increase the success rate of capturing their prey. They can be found hidden underneath branches. Their leaf-like or branch-like colors help them masquerade. Other species with bright and colorful colors can be found hidden beneath flowers. When hummingbirds are approaching, they are preparing for the attack. The attack can happen in such a short time that often the hummingbird is unable to avoid it.

But camouflage will not always work. Some species have developed keen vision to counter the camouflage. Chameleons are also known for their camouflage ability.

They use coloration to camouflage themselves. Their tongue can be quite a powerful tool. It can attack insects, such as mantises in a second. The camouflage used by mantises will not work in most circumstances. Before the insect is aware of the attack, the tongue touches the body of the insect and by the time we know it, they are in the mouth of the chameleon. Perhaps in the eyes of the predator, the ability to camouflage is just a way to earn yourself a few more days to live, especially when most defense mechanisms like camouflage won't work for predators. It's just some lame stunt.

PART 01 個人喜好

PART 02 二選一話題

PART 03 概述觀點

PART 04 整合文章和講座

PART 05 討論解決辦法

PART 06 概括講座內容

整合能力強化 ❷：閱讀與寫作

・請看著下列中文敘述，並將其「翻譯」成英文。

　　今天我們會涵蓋的部分是我一直想要討論的部分。偽裝。偽裝是自然界中很棒的機制。昆蟲，例如螳螂使用偽裝來使得它們在獵物或它們捕食者中較不顯眼。這會大幅增加它們捕捉獵物的成功率。它們藏於樹枝下方。它們像枯葉或像樹枝顏色幫助它們偽裝。其他物種有著光亮或鮮豔的顏色能藏於花朵下方。當蜂鳥靠近食，它們會準備攻擊機會。攻擊的時間能發生於很短的時間內，通常蜂鳥無法避開掉。

　　但是偽裝並不總是能發揮作用。其他物種可能可以發展出很敏銳的視野來應對這樣的偽裝。變色龍以它們的偽裝能力聞名。它們使用顏色來偽裝它們自己。它們的舌頭可以是相當強大的工具。它可以攻擊昆蟲，例如螳螂，在一秒內。螳螂使用的偽裝在大多數情況下是沒辦法發揮作用的。在昆蟲能察覺出攻擊前，舌頭觸碰到昆蟲的身體上，而接下來我們知道的是他們在變色龍的嘴巴裡了。或許對於捕食者的眼中，偽裝的能力只是一個讓你自己能多活幾天的伎倆，特別是當大多數的防護機制像是偽裝對捕食者發揮不了作用的時候。這只是一些不堪一擊的伎倆。

整合能力強化 ❸：閱讀、口說和口譯

・請看著下列中文敘述，並將其「口譯」成英文。

　　教授使用昆蟲作為解釋偽裝概念的例子。螳螂使用偽裝使它們在它們的捕食者眼中較不顯眼，所以它們能夠有更高的生存率。有些使用顏色作為偽裝的方式。蜂鳥通常無力察覺出螳螂靠近它們。

　　其他物種，例如變色龍也使用顏色來保護它們自己。但是由螳螂所使用的顏色對變色龍來說沒有用，因為變色龍的攻擊常來的太快了，在獵物能察覺之前。像教授在結尾所說的，「偽裝的能力只是一個讓你自己能多活幾天的伎倆，特別是當大多數的防護機制像是偽裝對捕食者發揮不了作用的時候。這只是一些不堪一擊的伎倆。」

PART 01 個人喜好

PART 02 二選一話題

PART 03 概述觀點

PART 04 整合文章和講座

PART 05 討論解決辦法

PART 06 概括講座內容

2 Myxoma virus

生物學：黏液瘤病毒

Narrator: in this question, you will listen to part of a lecture. Then you will be asked a question about it. After the question, you will have 20 seconds to prepare and 60 seconds to respond. **MP3 092**

Narrator: now listen to part of a talk in a biology class

☆ 筆記

PART 01 個人喜好

PART 02 二選一話題

PART 03 概述觀點

PART 04 整合文章和講座

PART 05 討論解決辦法

PART 06 概括講座內容

Explain how the story from the professor's lecture tells us something about European rabbits and Myxoma virus. ▶MP3 093

Preparation Time: 30 seconds
Response Time: 60 seconds

_____

_____

_____

_____

_____

_____

_____

_____

（準備期間內，試著在筆記欄頁上寫下幾個所想要描述的重點並搭配前面閱讀和所聽到的內容，做出接下來的回答。）

聽力原文 和中譯

Sinister rabbits in in the mind of people vary, according to customs or culture. Contrary to popular belief, adorable rabbits are such hateful creatures in the mind of most Australians. It's not some shocking news. But it somehow brings us to the Myxoma virus, the virus eventually used to control the population of the rabbits.

　　根據習俗或文化，在人們心中，對於感到邪惡的動物會因人而異。與現今流行的看法不同的是，可愛的兔子在大多數澳洲人眼中是如此令人憎恨的生物。這不是令人震驚的新聞。但是或多或少引起我們去關注黏液瘤病毒，這個病毒最終用於控制兔子的族群。

Hundreds of years ago, European rabbits arrived in the land of the paradise, Australia, since there were no predators, such as foxes, wolves, and so on. Breeding led to uncontrollable expansion of rabbits in Australia. The situation went a bit out of control. Australian animals were relatively mild, which led to their inability to compete with the so-called invasive species, the European rabbits. Starvation occurred among most Australian animals. Apart from the starvation, the ecological loss was unbearable.

PART 01　個人喜好
PART 02　二選一話題
PART 03　概述觀點
PART 04　整合文章和講座
PART 05　討論解決辦法
PART 06　概括講座內容

數百年前，歐洲兔子抵達的天堂之地，澳洲，牠們沒有天敵，像是狐狸、狼等等的。這個繁殖導致了兔子於澳洲無止盡地擴張。這個情況失去了控制。澳洲動物相對地溫馴，導致了牠們無力與所謂的外來物種，歐洲兔子競爭。飢餓的情況發生在大多數澳洲動物身上。除了飢餓之外，生態上的損失也無法忍受。

Eventually a lot of methods, such as poisonous gases and foxes were used to kill rabbits. Surprisingly, foxes were more inclined to eat sluggish Australian animals. Biocontrol seemed to be the only way out. The government introduced the Myxoma virus, the virus only fatal to European rabbits not American rabbits, and the virus has selectivity so that it is totally harmless to local farm animals and humans. The virus is the solution for the increasingly rampant rabbit population.

最終許多方法，例如有毒的氣體和狐狸用於獵殺兔子。令人感到驚訝地是，狐狸較傾向於食用懶散的澳洲動物。生物控制似乎是唯一的解決之道。政府引進了黏液瘤病毒，這個病毒只對歐洲兔子致命，但對美國兔子無害，這個病毒有了選擇性所以他對於當地的農業動物和人們無害。這個病毒是兔子族群逐漸猖獗的解決之道。

♡ 回說參考答案 和中譯　▶MP3 094

　　The professor explains the concept of biocontrol and the Myxoma virus through the story-telling way. People have their own sinister animals in mind. Some hate tarantulas, other dislike bats. In the mind of most Australians, it's the rabbit. Rabbits have caused more harm than we can even imagine. They had no predators when arrived on the land of Australia. The situation went out of control. The expansion of rabbits makes Australian animals less competitive and it led to the starvation and ecological losses in the country. Fortunately, the government has come up with using the virus to control the situation so the rabbit population is within control.

　　教授解釋了生物控制的概念和黏液瘤病毒透過說故事的方式。人們心中有他們感到邪惡的生物。有些討厭狼蛛，其他討厭蝙蝠。在大多數澳洲人心中，是兔子。兔子已經導致我們所能想像的危害。當牠們抵達澳洲這塊土地時牠們沒有天敵。情況失去了控制。兔子的擴張使得澳洲動物較不具競爭力，而且這導致了這個國家內飢餓和生態損失。幸運地是，政府已經想出使用病毒來控制這個情況，所以兔子族群在有效的控制範圍內。

PART 01 個人喜好

PART 02 二選一話題

PART 03 概述觀點

PART 04 整合文章和講座

PART 05 討論解決辦法

PART 06 概括講座內容

影子跟讀：看參考答案，並對於聽力原文做影子跟讀練習，提升主題答題並利用口說和聽力的關聯性強化聽力能力。

Sinister rabbits in the mind of people vary, according to customs or culture. Contrary to popular belief, adorable rabbits are such hateful creatures in the mind of most Australians. It's not some shocking news. But it somehow brings us to the Myxoma virus, the virus eventually used to control the population of the rabbits.

Hundreds of years ago, European rabbits arrived in the land of the paradise, Australia, since there were no predators, such as foxes, wolves, and so on. Bleeding led to uncontrollable expansion of rabbits in Australia. The situation went a bit out of control. Australian animals were relatively mild, which led to their inability to compete with the so-called invasive species, the European rabbits. Starvation occurred among most Australian animals. Apart from the starvation, the ecological loss was unbearable.

Eventually a lot of methods, such as poisonous gases and foxes were used to kill rabbits. Surprisingly, foxes were more inclined to eat sluggish Australian animals.

Biocontrol seemed to be the only way out. The government introduced the Myxoma virus, the virus only fatal to European rabbits not American rabbits, and the virus has selectivity so that it is totally harmless to local farm animals and humans. The virus is the solution for the increasingly rampant rabbit population.

 整合能力強化 ❷：閱讀、口說和口譯

· **請看著下列中文敘述，並將其「口譯」成英文。**

　　教授解釋了生物控制的概念和黏液瘤病毒透過說故事的方式。人們心中有牠們感到邪惡的生物。有些討厭狼蛛，其他討厭蝙蝠。在大多數澳洲人心中，是兔子。兔子已經導致我們所能想像的危害。當牠們抵達澳洲這塊土地時牠們沒有天敵。情況失去了控制。兔子的擴張使得澳洲動物較不具競爭力，而且這導致了這個國家內飢餓和生態損失。幸運地是，政府已經想出使用病毒來控制這個情況，所以兔子族群在有效的控制範圍內。

PART 01 個人喜好

PART 02 二選一話題

PART 03 概述觀點

PART 04 整合文章和講座

PART 05 討論解決辦法

PART 06 概括講座內容

3 Mass Whale Stranding
生態學：鯨魚集體擱淺

Narrator: in this question, you will listen to part of a lecture. Then you will be asked a question about it. After the question, you will have 20 seconds to prepare and 60 seconds to respond. **MP3 095**

Narrator: now listen to part of a talk in an ecology class

☆ 筆記

PART 01 個人喜好

PART 02 二選一話題

PART 03 概述觀點

PART 04 整合文章和講座

PART 05 討論解決辦法

PART 06 概括講座內容

Explain how the example from the professor's lecture tells us something about the possible reasons that those whales strand. ▶MP3 096

Preparation Time: 30 seconds
Response Time: 60 seconds

_____

_____

_____

_____

_____

_____

_____

_____

（準備期間內，試著在筆記欄頁上寫下幾個所想要描述的重點並搭配前面閱讀和所聽到的內容，做出接下來的回答。）

📻 **聽力原文 和中譯**

The blue ocean gradually turning red makes most of us worried about the fate of the whale population. Human interaction has interfered species in so many ways.

藍色的海洋逐漸變為紅色使得我們大多數的人都對於鯨魚族群感到擔憂。人類互動在許多面向上已經干擾到物種。

After that, not long ago, in western Australia, they found a mass whale stranding, which astounded the viewers. There were 150 whales, and among them 145 died eventually, and it is quite possible that they will re-strand themselves. While it remains a mystery why they would strand themselves in shallow waters. Let's take a look at the possible reasons that they strand themselves.

在那之後，不久前，在西澳，他們發現了鯨魚大量擱淺，這使得許多觀看者感到吃驚。數量是150隻鯨魚，在這之中最終有145隻鯨魚死亡，而且牠們相當有可能再次擱淺。雖然為什麼牠們會在淺水水域擱淺，這仍存謎，讓我們看下牠們擱淺最可能的原因。

PART 01 個人喜好

PART 02 二選一話題

PART 03 概述觀點

PART 04 整合文章和講座

PART 05 討論解決辦法

PART 06 概括講座內容

Environmental experts attribute mass strandings to four reasons. Human noise, being a social animal, sickness, and environmental pollution. Underwater sonar can be a huge disturbance for whales leading to disorientation and stranding in shallow water. They are gregarious animals. It's likely that they notice any distress call from their mates. In addition, they live collectively to increase the survival rate. The sickness of the whale which leads the team would cause the mass stranding. Finally, the environmental pollution. Worst weather conditions, oil leakage, and harmful algae are the reasons they strand. Whatever the reasons behind the stranding or whether the mass carcasses are caused by humans or non-humans, we, as human beings, owe them a clean place to live…and ensure they thrive…

環境專家將集體擱淺的原因歸於四項。人類噪音、社會性動物、疾病和環境汙染。水下聲納對於鯨魚來説會是個很大的干擾，牠們會失去方向而且擱淺在淺水水域。牠們是群居動物。牠們注意到同伴傳來的擾人的呼叫是很有可能的原因。此外，牠們集體生活以增加牠們的生存率。領導團隊的鯨魚的生病可能會導致集體擱淺。最後，環境汙染。最糟的天氣情況、漏油和有害的藻類都是牠們擱淺的原因。不論擱淺背後的原因或是不管是集體屍體是由人為或非人為因素，我們，充當人類，欠他們一個乾淨的地方生活...而且確保牠們繁殖下去。

PART 01 個人喜好
PART 02 二選一話題
PART 03 概述觀點
PART 04 整合文章和講座
PART 05 討論解決辦法
PART 06 概括講座內容

♡ 口說參考答案 和中譯   ▶MP3 097

The professor talks about the slaughter of whales and the mass whale stranding. We cannot help but feel worried for the whale population. Human activities have certainly caused some harm to lots of creatures. The mass whale stranding has led us to think about possible reasons behind the stranding. The professor mentions about the four possible reasons given by the environmental experts. Human noises, being a social animal, sickness, and environmental pollution. Noises make them disoriented, and living collectively makes them more easily stranded, if they are following the lead. Environmental pollution involves other three reasons, worst weather conditions, oil leakage, and detrimental algae. Whatever the reasons behind their stranding, we owe them an unpolluted place to live.

　　教授談論了鯨魚的屠殺和集體鯨魚的擱淺。我們無法不替整個鯨魚的族群感到擔憂。人類活動已經確實造成對許多生物的有些危害。集體鯨魚擱淺已經導致我們去思考擱淺背後的可能原因。教授提到關於四項由環境專家給予的原因。人類噪音、身為社會性動物、疾病和環境汙染。噪音使牠們失去方向，而且集體生活使牠們更易於擱淺，如果牠們遵照領頭鯨走。環境污染包含其他三項原因，惡劣的天氣情況、漏油和有害的藻類。不論擱淺背後的原因為何，我們都欠鯨魚一個未受污染的地方生活。

影子跟讀：看參考答案，並對於聽力原文做影子跟讀練習，提升主題答題並利用口說和聽力的關聯性強化聽力能力。

The blue ocean gradually turning red makes most of us worried about the fate of the whale population. Human interaction has interfered species in so many ways.

After that, not long ago, in western Australia, they found a mass whale stranding, which astounded the viewers. There were 150 whales, and among them 145 died eventually, and it is quite possible that they will re-strand themselves. While it remains a mystery why they would strand themselves in shallow waters. Let's take a look at the possible reasons that they strand.

Environmental experts attribute mass strandings to four reasons. Human noise, being a social animal, sickness, and environmental pollution. Underwater sonar can be a huge disturbance for whales leading to disorientation and stranding in. They are gregarious animals. It's likely that they notice any distress call from their mates. In addition, they live collectively to increase their survival rate. The sickness of the whale which leads the team would cause the mass stranding. Finally, the environmental pollution. Worst weather conditions, oil leakage, and harmful algae are the reasons they strand. Whatever the reasons behind the stranding or whether the mass carcasses are caused by humans or non-humans, we, as human beings, owe them a clean place to live…and ensure they thrive…

 整合能力強化 ❷：閱讀、口說和口譯

・**請看著下列中文敘述，並將其「口譯」成英文。**

　　教授談論了鯨魚的屠殺和集體鯨魚的擱淺。我們無法不替整個鯨魚的族群感到擔憂。人類活動已經確實造成對許多生物的有些危害。集體鯨魚擱淺已經導致我們去思考擱淺背後的可能原因。教授提到關於四項由環境專家給予的原因。人類噪音、身為社會性動物、疾病和環境汙染。噪音使牠們失去方向，而且集體生活使牠們更易於擱淺，如果牠們遵照領頭鯨走。環境污染包含其他三項原因，惡劣的天氣情況、漏油和有害的藻類。不論擱淺背後的原因為何，我們都欠鯨魚一個未受污染的地方生活。

PART 01 個人喜好
PART 02 二選一話題
PART 03 概述觀點
PART 04 整合文章和講座
PART 05 討論解決辦法
PART 06 概括講座內容

4

Habit
心理學課：習慣

Narrator: in this question, you will listen to part of a lecture. Then you will be asked a question about it. After the question, you will have 20 seconds to prepare and 60 seconds to respond. **MP3 098**

Narrator: now listen to part of a talk in a **psychology** class

☆ **筆記**

 口說 回答

Explain how the example from the professor's lecture gives us another idea about the influence of the habit
▶MP3 099

Preparation Time: 30 seconds
Response Time: 60 seconds

（準備期間內，試著在筆記欄頁上寫下幾個所想要描述的重點並搭配前面閱讀和所聽到的內容，做出接下來的回答。）

聽力原文 和中譯

Habits are one of the most important things we often overlook. We focus on so many things that we hardly take a look at them. In life, our success is heavily influenced by our habits whether they are good or bad. Each day we wake up at a specific time. We do a certain thing right after we get out of bed. Some take a walk. Others drink a glass of water. Still others brush their teeth. Of course, we cannot quite explain why certain people do particular things right after waking up or right after they park their car. We can be certain that all small actions of ours affect what we will become in the future.

習慣是我們通常忽略的大多數重要的事情之一。我們將焦點放在許多事情上，以至於我們幾乎沒有注意到他們。在生活中，我們的成功受到我們習慣很大程度地影響，不論是好或是壞。每天我們在特定的時間起床。在我們下床後，我們需要做特定的事情。有些則是走段路。其他人則喝杯水。而還有其他人則刷牙。當然我們不可能去解釋為什麼特定人會再起床後及停車後做某些特殊的事情。我們可以確定的是我們所有的小行為都影響著我們會在未來成為什麼樣的人。

PART 01 個人喜好
PART 02 二選一話題
PART 03 概述觀點
PART 04 整合文章和講座
PART 05 討論解決辦法
PART 06 概括講座內容

The person who develops the habit of going to the office an hour early and then reading the newspaper will eventually be an early bird in the office and have a reading habit before he starts to work. He will have plenty of time to think and meditate. By contrast, another person who arrives at the office at a much later time will not feel as poised. It is these small things that we should attention to. The power of habits can turn us into a pretty successful person or the person who still dreams about being one one day.

　　一個人培養出每天提早一小時到辦公室的習慣和緊接著看著報紙會最終成了辦公室的早鳥，而且在他開始工作前有著閱讀習慣。他將有著充足的時間去思考和沉思。相對之下，另一個人抵達到辦公室的時間是相對晚些，則不會有著相對沉靜的感受。這就是我們需要注意的些微的小事情。習慣的力量能將我們改造成一位相當成功的人士或是只是夢想著有天我們能成為成功人士。

♡ 回說參考答案 和中譯　　▶MP3 100

PART 01 個人喜好
PART 02 二選一話題
PART 03 概述觀點
PART 04 整合文章和講座
PART 05 討論解決辦法
PART 06 概括講座內容

The professor talks about the importance of habits. Through the explanation, we can gradually understand the essence of the habits. It's right after the time we wake up. It's the little things we do that make the difference. While we cannot quite explain why people do particular things after we wake up, changing the habit can make a big difference. The professor uses the example of the person who goes to work an hour early and the person who goes to work at a much later time to explain the difference. We can be the former, who eventually becomes the successful person, or the latter, the one who still dreams about being one.

　　教授談論了習慣的重要性。透過解釋，我們可以逐漸了解到習慣的本質。緊接在我們起床後的時段。是這些小事情讓我們有所不同。雖然我們某種程度上去解釋，在起床後人們為什麼做特定的事情，改變習慣能產生顯著的差異。教授使用了一個每天提到一小時到辦公室的人和一位每天較晚些時段才到辦公室的人解釋這樣所造成的差異性。我們可以成為前者，當個最終成為成功人士者，或者是後者，一位總是夢想能成為成功人士的人。

整合能力強化 ❶：口說與聽力

影子跟讀：看參考答案，並對於聽力原文做影子跟讀練習，提升主題答題並利用口說和聽力的關聯性強化聽力能力。

Habits are one of the most important things we often overlook. We focus on so many things that we hardly take a look at them. In life, our success is heavily influenced by our habits whether they are good or bad. Each day we wake up at a specific time. We do a certain thing right after we get out of bed. Some take a walk. Others drink a glass of water. Still others brush their teeth. Of course, we cannot quite explain why certain people do particular things right after waking up or right after they park their car. We can be certain that all small actions of ours affect what we will become in the future.

The person who develops the habit of going to the office an hour early and then reading the newspaper will eventually be an early bird in the office and have a reading habit before he starts to work. He will have plenty of time to think and meditate. By contrast, another person who arrives at the office at a much later time will not feel as poised. It is these small things that we should pay attention to. The power of habits can turn us into a pretty successful person or the person who still dreams about being one one day.

整合能力強化 ❷：閱讀與寫作

・請看著下列中文敘述，並將其「翻譯」成英文。

　　習慣是我們通常忽略的大多數重要的事情之一。我們將焦點放在許多事情上，以至於我們幾乎沒有注意到他們。在生活中，我們的成功受到我們習慣很大程度地影響，不論是好或是壞。每天我們在特定的時間起床。在我們下床後，我們需要做特定的事情。有些則是走段路。其他人則喝杯水。而還有其他人則刷牙。當然我們不可能去解釋為什麼特定人會再起床後及停車後做某些特殊的事情。我們可以確定的是我們所有的小行為都影響著我們會在未來成為什麼樣的人。

　　一個人培養出每天提早一小時到辦公室的習慣和緊接著看著報紙會最終成了辦公室的早鳥，而且在他開始工作前有著閱讀習慣。他將有著充足的時間去思考和沉思。相對之下，另一個人抵達到辦公室的時間是相對晚些，則不會有著相對沉靜的感受。這就是我們需要注意的些微的小事情。習慣的力量能將我們改造成一位相當成功的人士或是只是夢想著有天我們能成為成功人士。

PART 01 個人喜好

PART 02 二選一話題

PART 03 概述觀點

PART 04 整合文章和講座

PART 05 討論解決辦法

PART 06 概括講座內容

Narrator: in this question, you will listen to part of a lecture. Then you will be asked a question about it. After the question, you will have 20 seconds to prepare and 60 seconds to respond. **MP3 101**

Narrator: now listen to part of a talk in a geography class

⭐ 筆記

PART 01 個人喜好

PART 02 二選一話題

PART 03 概述觀點

PART 04 整合文章和講座

PART 05 討論解決辦法

PART 06 概括講座內容

 口說 回答

Explain how the story from the professor's lecture tells us about the Mara river and African animals' migration

▶ MP3 102

Preparation Time: 30 seconds
Response Time: 60 seconds

_____

_____

_____

_____

_____

_____

_____

_____

（準備期間內，試著在筆記欄頁上寫下幾個所想要描述的重點並搭配前面閱讀和所聽到的內容，做出接下來的回答。）

聽力原文 和中譯

The Mara river is one of the well-known rivers in the world. it is also known as Africa's blood river. The blood uncovers the story behind. It's not just a river in the geographical sense. It symbolizes the life of African animals undergoing migration during which they have to pass through a river, but it's not as easy as it seems. River torrents are not merciful to animals which pass through the river. Young African animals without a robust body are not able to withstand the torrents. Apart from the natural forces, such as river torrents and stiff cliffs near the river bank, wildebeests, zebras, and other herbivores have a far bigger concern, the Nile crocodiles hidden beneath the river. Crocodiles grasp every chance to grab animals which just jump into the river. Some end up being their victims. The migration is quite breathtaking and a large scale one.

馬拉河是世界上知名的河流之一。這條河流也稱作是非洲的血河。血液則揭露著背後的故事。這不僅僅是條河流，以地理感受來說。它象徵著非洲的動物們經歷著他們遷徙的旅程，期間牠們經過這條河流，但是卻不似表面上看的那樣簡單。河流中的激流對於通過這條河流的動物沒有那麼仁慈。年輕的非洲生物沒有強健的身軀無法抵抗激流。除了自然的力量，像是河流的激流和靠近河岸的陡峭岩壁外，牛羚、斑馬和其他草食

PART 01 個人喜好

PART 02 二選一話題

PART 03 概述觀點

PART 04 整合文章和講座

PART 05 討論解決辦法

PART 06 概括講座內容

性動物有著更大的考量在，尼羅河鱷魚藏在河流中。鱷魚抓緊每個機會抓住往河裡跳的動物。有些最終成了犧牲者。這個遷徙是相當令人屏息的而且是很大規模的。

According to a survey, only 30% of animals can successfully return to the place of departure. Somehow the mechanism of the natural forces is doing their work to maintain the number to a certain amount, and brings the food to carnivores such as crocodiles, lions, and cheetahs. The dry season is the hidden force which creates this magnificent view at the Mara river.

根據這個調查，僅有30%的動物能夠成功地回到出發的地點。有點像是天然的力量在執行牠們該作的事，維持動物數量在某個數量，而這是替肉食性動物，像是鱷魚、獅子和獵豹帶來了食物。乾季是創造馬拉河這個壯麗景觀的隱藏力量。

PART 01 個人喜好

PART 02 二選一話題

PART 03 概述觀點

PART 04 整合文章和講座

PART 05 討論解決辦法

PART 06 概括講座內容

♡ 口說參考答案 和中譯　▶MP3 103

　　In describing the Mara river, the professor tells us the nickname of the river and the migration story of the river. Lots of herbivores join the journey of the migration due to the dry season. They are forced to leave a land without grasses and enough water resources. Passing through the river is not as easy as it seems. Natural forces and hidden dangers are waiting for the animals. River torrents and crocodiles are not merciful. They act like cruel masters in this migration. When the journey is finished, only 30% of the animals can successfully return to the departure place. It is this migration that creates such an amazing view of the Mara river.

　　在描述馬拉河，教授告訴我們河流的暱稱和這條河流的遷徙故事。因為乾季，許多草食性動物都參加了這個旅程。牠們被迫要離開沒有草的土地和為了充足的水資源。通過這條河流沒有看起來那樣簡單。天然的力量和隱藏的危險都等著動物。河流的激流和鱷魚都沒有那麼仁慈。牠們充當這個遷徙中殘酷的主宰者。到旅程結束後，僅有30%的動物能夠成功地回到出發的地點。是這個遷徙過程替馬拉河創造了驚人的景色。

影子跟讀：看參考答案，並對於聽力原文做影子跟讀練習，提升主題答題並利用口說和聽力的關聯性強化聽力能力。

The Mara river is one of the well-known rivers in the world. it is also known as Africa's blood river. The blood uncovers the story behind. It's not just a river in the geographical sense. It symbolizes the life of African animals undergoing migration during which they have to pass through a river, but it's not as easy as it seems. River torrents are not merciful to animals which pass through the river. Young African animals without a robust body are not able to withstand the torrents. Apart from the natural forces, such as river torrents and stiff cliffs near the river bank, wildebeests, zebras, and other herbivores have a far bigger concern, the Nile crocodiles hidden beneath the river. Crocodiles grasp every chance to grab animals which just jump into the river. Some end up being their victims. The migration is quite breathtaking and a large scale one.

According to a survey, only 30% of animals can successfully return to the place of departure. Somehow the mechanism of the natural forces is doing their work to maintain the number to a certain amount, and brings food to carnivores such as crocodiles, lions, and cheetahs. The dry season is the hidden force which creates this magnificent view at the Mara river.

 整合能力強化 ❷：閱讀與寫作

・**請看著下列中文敘述，並將其「翻譯」成英文。**

　　馬拉河是世界上知名的河流之一。這條河流也稱作是非洲的血河。血液則揭露著背後的故事。這不僅僅是條河流，以地理感受來説。它象徵著非洲的動物們經歷著他們遷徙的旅程，期間牠們經過這條河流，但是卻不似表面上看的那樣簡單。河流中的激流對於通過這條河流的動物沒有那麼仁慈。年輕的非洲生物沒有強健的身軀無法抵抗激流。除了自然的力量，像是河流的激流和靠近河岸的陡峭岩壁外，牛羚、斑馬和其他草食性動物有著更大的考量在，尼羅河鱷魚藏在河流中。鱷魚抓緊每個機會抓住往河裡跳的動物。有些最終成了犧牲者。這個遷徙是相當令人屏息的而且是很大規模的。

　　根據這個調查，僅有30%的動物能夠成功地回到出發的地點。有點像是天然的力量在執行牠們該作的事，維持動物數量在某個數量，而這是替肉食性動物，像是鱷魚、獅子和獵豹帶來了食物。乾季是創造馬拉河這個壯麗景觀的隱藏力量。

01 PART 個人喜好

02 PART 二選一話題

03 PART 概述觀點

04 PART 整合文章和講座

05 PART 討論解決辦法

06 PART 概括講座內容

315

新托福口說參考資料和引用

參考資料：

● 《iBT托福口語全方位解析》
   湯蕾、賈青帆・中國大陸：中國人民大學出版社

● 《不是權威不出書：托福命題總監教你征服新托福閱讀聽力》
   秦蘇珊（2014）・台北：捷徑文化

● 網址 https://www.youtube.com/watch?v=INYFYq_D_Xc

引用說明：

Part 4 unit 4 https://zh.wikipedia.org/zh-tw/%E7%A6%8F%E5%AF%BF%E8%9E%BA
Part 6 unit 2 https://hottopic.chinatimes.com/20151223002843-260812
Part 6 unit 3 https://www.thenewslens.com/article/92273
Part 6 unit 5 http://africa.go2c.info/view.php?doc=WildebeestMigration

p.54
參考書籍 *Grinding It Out*
引述句子 Nothing in the world can take place of persistence.
          (Ray and Robert, 2016, p.195)

p.175
參考書籍 *Originals*
引述句子 Procrastination might be conducive to originality.
          (Adam, 2016, p.94)

p.178
參考書籍 *Originals*
引述句子 Procrastination may be the enemy of productivity, but it can be a resource
          of creativity.
          (Adam, 2016, p.95)

用最瑣碎的時間 建立學習自信
輕鬆打下英語學習基礎！

■用心智圖概念，圖「解」複雜又難吸收的文法觀念
■30天學習進度規劃，不出國也能變身ABC
■規劃三大階段學習法，拋開制式學習，更有成效！

英文文法超圖解　　　定價 NT$ 369
ISBN：9789869528825
書系編號：文法/生活英語系列 005
書籍規格：386頁/18K/普通級/雙色印刷/平裝

說文解詩學文法　「戀」習英語寫作

精選「經典」英美情詩附中英對照，引用的詩句對應文法
概念，並且提供英語寫作範文與中譯，幫助讀者掌握寫作
起、承、轉、合的訣竅，優雅閱讀同時提升寫作功力！

學文法，戀習英語寫作　　　定價 NT$ 369
ISBN：9789869285544
書系編號：Learn Smart 062
書籍規格：304頁/18K/普通級/雙色印刷/平裝

結合英、法語字彙　享受甜點＋下午茶
語言學習的多重樂趣

精選與甜點、下午茶有關的英文字彙，皆附例句以及法語
字彙，且由專業錄音老師錄製英文單字、例句和法語單字
，學會最正統的發音！特別企劃【魔法廚房】由前輩親授
製作甜點的秘訣與心得，提供調整、創新口味的建議，幫
助店家製作出口感更符合東方人的點心，提高自家產品的
接受度與流行度！

Bon Appetit 甜點物語：英法語字彙 (附MP3)定價 NT$ 360
ISBN：9789869285582
書系編號：Learn Smart 065
書籍規格：288頁/18K/普通級/雙色印刷/平裝附光碟

─ 親子英語 ─

在家就能輕鬆打造親子英語教室
小學生必備的基礎學科通通有

將家庭教育、英語學習和學校課程巧妙融入本書，內容涵蓋天文、地理、生物、科學、人文藝術，主題引導學習，讓小朋友聽得懂，讀得下去。是兼具實用和趣味的親子英語共讀書。

我的第一本萬用親子英語 (附MP3)
定價 NT$ 399
ISBN：9789869528894
書系編號：文法/生活英語系列 006
書籍規格：224頁/18K/普通級/全彩印刷/平裝附光碟

結合自然發音與KK音標的圖解發音書
解決學習發音的困擾

單元特色：
◎50個音標+6組字尾聯音：迅速辨認音標與發音規則
◎8組繞口令：透過反覆練習繞口令，矯正英文發音，加強口齒伶俐度
◎老師獨門音節劃分法：劃分音節，輕鬆讀出英文長字

圖解英文發音二重奏：自然發音、KK音標 (附MP3)
定價 NT$ 369
ISBN：9789869191586
書系編號：Learn Smart 055
書籍規格：288頁/18K/普通級/雙色印刷/平裝附光碟

運用思考力、創意力和英語力
編織屬於自己的童話故事

加入許多科技元素、高科技產品於故事情節中，融入許多道地語彙及美式幽默，更將童話故事中人物善惡對調，kuso的情節激起許多風波和笑點，引領讀者品味不同的故事。學習另一種活潑、新穎的說法，讓你的口語英文更自然。

童話奇緣：Follow Kuso英語童話，來一場穿越時空之旅 (附MP3)
定價 NT$ 380
ISBN：9789869191555
書系編號：Learn Smart 052
書籍規格：332頁/18K/普通級/雙色印刷/平裝附光碟

── 心靈勵志 ──

凡人行走江湖，人情世故終究是冷暖自知
凡人精心佈局，只謂人生如戲又戲如人生
生活沒有優劣，皆是一種生命情境。作者將親眼見證的風景與感觸認真記下──
探究幾部經典，卻不在此評論文學；講述諸多影劇，但不在此寫作影評，
描繪各種日常，充滿了隨想與際遇，正因為電影和文學從未遠離過日常生活。

凡人佈局──內心戲現正熱映中　　定價 NT$ 320
ISBN：9789869644822
書系編號：好心情 007
書籍規格：256頁/25K/普通級/單色印刷/平裝

本書不是食譜，而是一本私房日記。
製作「有故事」的點心，比製作「漂亮」的點心更有趣
作者藉由製作甜鹹點，分享了她和親友間磨合與成長的記錄，亦開拓出自己的烘
焙學習之路。本書能滿足你的味蕾，富足你的心靈，既是新科家庭主婦的工具書
，更是異鄉遊子們的心靈雞湯。

食遇美國──固執台妹的異鄉冒險　　定價 NT$ 350
ISBN：9789869644815
書系編號：好心情 008
書籍規格：160頁/25K/普通級/全彩印刷/平裝

非關孕育，而是護育！珍惜生命、熱愛生命，來自你我有愛的心
集結各類寵物主人們撰寫的照料筆記，將飼主與寵物朝夕相處的情景透過文字呈
現，讓讀者體會到寵物所帶來的歡樂與撫慰人心的能量。亦提醒社會大眾，別讓
「領養代替購買」淪為愛心氾濫的口號，而是做為一種正在落實的生命態度。

寫給牠──最珍貴的朋友&家人　　定價 NT$ 320
ISBN：9789869644808
書系編號：好心情 006
書籍規格：160頁/25K/普通級/全彩印刷/平裝

過站不停！開往下一站── 再見青春，再見前任
若沒有飛鳥的失速流離，魚怎能學會離水呼吸？
若沒有魚的張望關注，飛鳥怎能學會低空飛行？若不是前任，
若不是那些曾經的不完美，我又怎能變得更完整美好？

致我們扭曲的記憶──前任　　定價 NT$ 299
ISBN：9789869366489
書系編號：好心情 004
書籍規格：224頁/25K/普通級/單色印刷/平裝

國家圖書館出版品預行編目(CIP)資料

新托福100+ iBT 口說 / 韋爾著.
-- 初版. -- 臺北市：倍斯特, 2018.12　面；
公分. --（考用英語系列；14）
ISBN 978-986-96309-8-6（平裝附光碟）
1.托福考試

805.1894　　　　　　　　　107017869

考用英語 014

新托福100+iBT 口說(附MP3)

初　　版	2018年12月	
定　　價	新台幣429元	

作　　者	韋爾
出　　版	倍斯特出版事業有限公司
發 行 人	周瑞德
電　　話	886-2-2351-2007
傳　　真	886-2-2351-0887
地　　址	100 台北市中正區福州街1號10樓之2
E - m a i l	best.books.service@gmail.com
官　　網	www.bestbookstw.com
執行總監	齊心瑀
責任編輯	陳韋佑
封面構成	高鐘琪
內頁構成	菩薩蠻數位文化有限公司
印　　製	大亞彩色印刷製版股份有限公司

港澳地區總經銷	泛華發行代理有限公司
地　　址	香港新界將軍澳工業邨駿昌街7號2樓
電　　話	852-2798-2323
傳　　真	852-2796-5471